"I'm Not Very Good At This Kind Of Thing,"

Melina confessed.

"At what kind of thing?" Nick asked.

She sighed. "At the kind of thing that's supposed to happen between a man and a woman."

"Meaning?"

"Clever repartee… Flirting. Dating. Kissing. Making out…" Her voice grew strained. "Not to mention whatever comes after that."

"What are you trying to tell me, Melina?"

"I want to kiss you—"

"But—"

"What I'm trying to tell you, Nick, is that I'm not very good at kissing, but I think I could be."

"In other words, you have potential."

"Exactly." Melina swallowed hard. "And I thought you might help me get started."

Dear Reader,

Just when you thought Mother Nature had turned up the heat, along comes Silhouette Desire to make things even *hotter*. It's June...the days are longer, the kids are out of school, and we've got the very best that romance has to offer.

Let's start with our *Man of the Month, Haven's Call,* which is by Robin Elliott, a writer many of you have written to tell me is one of your favorites.

Next, we have *Salty and Felicia* by Lass Small. If you've ever wondered how those two older Browns got together, well, now you'll get to find out! From Jennifer Greene comes the latest installment in her JOCK'S BOYS series, *Bewildered.* And Suzanne Simms's series, HAZARDS, INC., continues with *The Pirate Princess.*

Anne Marie Winston has created a tender, wonderful story, *Substitute Wife.* And if you like drama and intensity with your romance, don't miss Lucy Gordon's *Uncaged!*

It just doesn't get any better than this...so read and enjoy.

All the best,

Lucia Macro
Senior Editor

Please address questions and book requests to:
Reader Service
U.S.: P.O. Box 1325, Buffalo, NY 14269
Canadian: P.O. Box 1050, Niagara Falls, Ont. L2E 7G7

SUZANNE SIMMS

THE PIRATE PRINCESS

ISBN 0-373-05862-4

THE PIRATE PRINCESS

This edition published by arrangement with Harlequin Enterprises B. V.

Printed in U.S.A.

Books by Suzanne Simms

Silhouette Desire

Moment in Time #9
Of Passion Born #17
A Wild, Sweet Magic #43
All Night Long #61
So Sweet a Madness #79
Only this Night #109
Dream Within a Dream #150
Nothing Ventured #258
Moment of Truth #299
Not His *Wedding!* #718
Not Her *Wedding!* #754
**The Brainy Beauty* #850
**The Pirate Princess* #862

*Hazards, Inc.

SUZANNE SIMMS

had her first romance novel published fourteen years ago and is "thrilled" to be writing again for Silhouette Desire. Suzanne has traveled extensively, including a memorable trip to the Philippines, which, she says, "changed my life." She also writes historical romances as Suzanne Simmons. She currently lives with her husband, her son and her cat, Merlin, in Fort Wayne, Indiana.

"Diamonds are a girl's best friend."
For Stella Cameron, one of the "diamonds" in my life.

One

He was big.

He was blond.

He was beautiful.

He was buck naked.

He was Neptune rising from the sea. He was Poseidon, worshiped by fishermen and sailors alike, the cause of storms, floods and earthquakes, able to raise whole islands from the bottom of the ocean with a single stroke of his trident. Only in this case the trident was a snorkel that he had removed and was carrying in one hand. It just covered him.

Inadvertently.

Strategically.

Luckily.

He didn't look like a pirate.

That was Melina Morgan's next thought. A pirate would have a shock of black hair and a black patch covering one eye. He would be dressed in black breeches that fit him like a glove and knee-high black boots. There would be a black stubble on his chiseled chin and, of course, a black expression on his devilishly handsome face.

He didn't look like a pirate because he wasn't a pirate. He was a beach bum. A ne'er-do-well. A surfer. A swimmer. A water-skier. One of those golden boys who played volleyball in the hot sand and sported a perfect tan year-round.

Greek god? Pirate? Beach boy? Melina made an expressive face. Maybe her mother and father were right. Maybe she had spent too much time holed up in the library, her nose in a book, or in the air daydreaming, spinning tales of romance, adventure and intrigue. Her parents often said she'd had a tendency toward the fanciful since she was a girl.

Well, she was all grown up now and she wasn't being fanciful and she wasn't daydreaming, Melina Morgan reminded herself as she watched the man. He was real. Very real. Every last *bare* inch of him.

She couldn't take her eyes off the man as he walked out of the ocean, the setting sun behind him. He hadn't spotted her yet. When he did, Melina knew what his first thought would be— How much could she see? Was he clearly visible, or was he merely a shadowy silhouette with the fading light of day behind him?

Everything.

She could see every last thing.

He was magnificent. His hair was blond, slightly long at the nape and dripping wet. It was matted to his head. Rivulets ran down his neck and shoulders and onto his bare chest.

He was tall—probably six-three, possibly six-four—broad-shouldered and muscular. There was a smattering of honey-colored hair in the center of his chest that fanned out to encircle two small, brown male nipples. There was more sun-kissed silky stuff on his forearms, arrowing down his taut torso, curling around his manhood—thankfully his lower body was partially obscured by the mask and snorkel—and glistening with seawater on the long, long legs that seemed to go on forever. Obviously he wasn't the kind of blonde who burned in the sun. He was a rich golden-brown all over.

Melina knew the exact moment he spotted her. The awareness and the surprise that followed were apparent in his intelligent golden-brown eyes. The next instant surprise was replaced by something else.

He opened his mouth. "This beach is private."

She sat up and gazed down the deserted stretch of sand with a nonchalance she was far from feeling. "It certainly is."

The man reached for the white towel she hadn't seen against the white sand, and unselfconsciously wrapped it around his hips. "I mean literally. This is a private beach. Reserved for these two cottages."

"I know."

He wrinkled his forehead. "Then what are you doing here?"

"Vacationing."

His tone was one of exasperation. "I didn't mean literally."

Melina made a motion with her arm. "I'm staying in the first cottage."

He bit off something that sounded like *son of a bitch.* "I beg your pardon."

"I said I'm staying at the pink cottage." She put her head back, shielded her eyes with one hand and squinted up at him. The man towered over her. "Simon said there would be no one else here."

"Simon said?"

"Simon Hazard. He owns the two cottages on this island."

"He also happens to own the whole island," the man informed her.

Melina slapped her forehead. "Of course. That explains why it's called Cayo Hazard."

"Brilliant deduction," muttered the blond giant.

She had assumed the waters were hazardous, or the reef treacherous—more than one Spanish galleon or English frigate must have sunk off these shores in their time—but it had not occurred to Melina that the island was named for her host.

"Cayo Hazard. Key Hazard. Simon Hazard," she murmured, thinking out loud.

"If I may ask, how do you know Simon?" demanded the looming figure.

The man was good-looking, but he had no manners. "You may ask. I may choose not to answer." She gave him the same pointed look she used to great advantage when reprimanding rowdy boys at the library. He simply stared back at her. Apparently the technique didn't work on overgrown boys. "Simon Hazard is one of the chief benefactors of the Moose Creek Municipal Library," she informed him.

"The Moose Creek Municipal Library?"

"Moose Creek, Wisconsin."

He scowled, then turned and gazed off toward the blue horizon for half a minute. "Cripes, it's another one of Simon's bloody bleeding-heart charities. I should have known."

Melina stiffened. "We were in dire straits."

"No doubt."

"He saved us from closing our doors."

"Sounds like something Simon would do."

"We had to have a new roof. The old one leaked like a sieve," Melina explained. Then she added, "Simon Hazard is a hero to the entire town of Moose Creek."

He looked at her, unimpressed. "Population one thousand?"

"Eight hundred, actually." The soft sand had worked its way beneath her swimsuit. Melina wiggled her bottom, but it only made matters worse. "How do you know Simon?"

"He's my uncle."

She arched a skeptical brow. "Uncle?" She had met Simon Hazard on several occasions. He was in his early thirties. This man had to be about the same age.

The blond beach bum blew out his breath. Melina sensed that he wasn't used to explaining himself to anyone—let alone a stranger. "It's one of those generational-gap things," he said inconclusively.

Her arched eyebrow went higher. "Really?"

"Really." He stood his ground. Silently. Then he shrugged his massive shoulders and went on. "My grandfather married five times and had five sons. My father is the eldest. Simon is the youngest. There's a thirty-year span between them. Actually I'm two years older than Simon."

"I see." The math worked out, but Melina still had her doubts.

Apparently the man decided to go on the offensive. "Simon didn't tell me you would be here."

"It must have slipped his mind."

"It must have."

Melina wasn't used to having her integrity questioned. "If you don't believe me, why don't you row your little boat over to Key West and call him?"

"Can't."

"Can't or won't?"

He shook his head back and forth, and made an impatient sound. "Wouldn't do any good. By now Simon is somewhere up in the hinterlands between Thailand and Burma."

"I thought Burma was called Myanmar now."

That brought a raised eyebrow. "It is. Most people simply aren't aware of the change."

"I'm not most people."

"What are you?" His voice and manner were sarcastic. "The Moose Creek municipal librarian?"

Melina's eyes widened behind her dark glasses. It wasn't as if the information were tattooed on her forehead. How had he guessed?

Then she let out a resigned sigh. Once a librarian, always a librarian, they said. It was a little—*a lot,* in Moose Creek—like being a nun. When people found out, they treated you differently.

"Yes, as a matter of fact, I am the librarian," she finally confessed.

A large, well-shaped hand was driven through still-damp hair. "Good grief, a librarian."

She quickly changed the subject. "I don't suppose they have telephones in the hinterlands of Myanmar."

"Lady, they don't even have two Dixie cups and a string." The man frowned and announced, "I don't like it."

"You don't like *what?*"

"Sharing my island."

"I thought you said it was Simon's island."

In response all he did was mutter, "Simon promised I would be by myself. This is the first vacation I've had in years, and what do I get?"

Melina was tempted to answer his question, but in the end she didn't.

His eyes narrowed suspiciously. "Who in the hell are you, anyway?"

It wasn't so much the man's rudeness that riled Melina; it was the fact that he acted as if he owned the whole darned world. Indeed, he'd had an "attitude" ever since he had walked out of the water with only a snorkel to cover his bare assets.

The good citizens of Moose Creek, Wisconsin, would have been shocked to hear their usually demure librarian fling back, "Just who in the hell are *you?*"

He was tempted not to tell her. But in the end he did. "Nicholas Hazard."

The young woman got to her feet, dusted the fine white sand off her derriere—and a very nice derriere, it was, too—shook out her towel, slipped her bare feet into the skimpy sandals that had been tossed onto the beach, pushed the long black hair out of her eyes and pulled on the strap of her black swimsuit. Then she took off her sunglasses and looked straight at him.

He was floored.

Blue.

Caribbean blue.

Nick didn't think he had ever seen anyone with eyes that color before. They were a brilliant combination of blue and violet and lavender and all the hues in between. Equally amazing, the lady librarian from Moose Creek seemed oblivious to the effect she had on him. In fact, she turned her back on him—something women in general didn't do with Nick—and started off down the beach toward the pink cottage.

He didn't shout. He raised his voice only enough to be heard. "I didn't catch the name."

She threw it over her shoulder. "Melina Morgan."

"As in Sir Henry Morgan, British buccaneer?"

The young woman appeared to stub her toe on something in the sand, no doubt a seashell or a rock or a piece of driftwood. "The very one."

"Do you scuba dive, Ms. Morgan?"

She paused, then swiveled on her heel. "No, I don't scuba dive."

Nick held up the equipment in his left hand. "By chance, do you snorkel?"

"No, I do not snorkel."

He deliberately gave her a long, measuring look. "I assume you know how to swim."

"There is very little need for swimming where I come from, Mr. Hazard. We have no ocean, no lake, no pond and no swimming pool."

The corners of his mouth lifted in a sardonic smile. "You do have bathtubs."

"We do have bathtubs. But rest assured, I always stay at the shallow end."

She was quick. He had to hand her that.

"There are a number of boats on Cayo Hazard, Ms. Morgan. You would be well advised not venture out on the water alone. The gulf and the Straits of Florida can both be deceptively treacherous to even the most experienced sailor."

"I can take care of myself."

"I've heard that before."

"I'm a big girl."

"Not that big." Nick guessed her to be a perfect thirty-four *B,* but he didn't say so aloud. Instead he ventured, "You can't be much more than five feet four inches tall."

"I'm five-five."

"As I said, not much more than five-four." He started with the tips of her toes—the nails were polished a powder-puff pink—and made his way, slowly, up to her face. He was very thorough. "I can't help wondering why you would choose to vacation on a Florida beach when you don't scuba dive, you don't snorkel, you don't swim and from the looks of your skin you don't even tan."

She stood there and stared at him.

"What *do* you do, Ms. Morgan?"

"I mind my own business." With that she turned and continued on her way.

Cheeky.

The girl was cheeky.

An unexpected smile momentarily broke the stern line of Nick's mouth. Ms. Morgan's swimsuit had a tendency to ride up in the back. She was cheeky, all right... and in all the right places.

He picked up his other belongings and started off toward his own cottage—the blue one.

Frankly he wasn't convinced the island was big enough for both of them. If Melina Morgan knew what was good for her, she'd stay out of his way. He was on holiday. The first holiday he'd had in years. The first holiday there had been time for since he and his half brother, Jonathan, had launched their company, Hazards, Inc.

He needed rest. He needed solitude. He needed peace and quiet.

He didn't need any complications, and he sure as hell didn't need a beautiful woman cluttering up his beach.

Two

He couldn't sleep.

Nick threw back the sheet and reached for the pair of denim cutoffs he had tossed over the wicker chair beside the bed. He slipped them on in a single motion. Then he pulled a faded blue T-shirt over his head, combed his fingers through his hair and rubbed his hand back and forth along his jaw. He hadn't shaved in a week. As a matter of fact, he hadn't bothered to pack a razor for this trip. It had seemed like a good idea at the time. Now he wasn't so sure.

"You need some fresh air, Hazard," he said as he thrust his bare feet into a pair of scruffy loafers, opened the paneled French doors that led to the patio and the garden beyond, and stepped outside.

He exhaled slowly and put his head back. Damned if the weather wasn't ideal.

The sky was a deep velvet blue punctuated with the lights of thousands of stars. The breeze off the ocean cooled the air and caressed the skin. The vegetation was thick and lush and fragrant. White ginger lilies grew along the pathway. Bright yellow hibiscus and deep purple bougainvillea cascaded over stone walls. Spanish moss grew in the shade of the trees that formed a canopy overhead.

He could hear the call of a night bird and the distant screech of a peacock, the singing of nocturnal insects and the familiar sound of waves washing onto shore.

"Just another perfect night in paradise," Nick muttered to himself.

He took a deep breath of sea air and gave the tropical hammock, hanging between two palm trees, a push with his hand as he strolled by.

What the hell was he doing here, anyway?

But he knew the answer to his own question. He was on holiday. He was vacationing. He was taking some time off. He was goofing off. He was doing nothing.

Nick scratched his head. He couldn't remember the last time he had done absolutely nothing.

It seemed his life had always had a purpose, a plan, a schedule. First there had been undergraduate school at Purdue University, then an advanced degree in engineering, then the navy. Five years spent as a navy SEAL, five more spent as a security consultant to oil-rich sheikhs and heads of state had pretty much taken up an entire decade.

In the line of duty he had traveled the world. He had learned about its customs, its languages, its people. He had experienced its beauty and its ugliness. In the end there was very little he hadn't seen or done.

Not that he was a careless man. Just the opposite was true. He was careful. Very careful. It was one reason he was alive to tell the tale.

When he'd returned to the States nearly three years ago, Nick had been at loose ends until his older brother, Jonathan, had come to him with the idea of Hazards, Inc.

"It's the best of both worlds," Jonathan had claimed. "We'll put our expertise to work, but we won't have to sleep in a strange bed every night, live out of a suitcase or eat on the run." His sibling had been very persuasive. "We will live," he had been promised, "like normal people."

"Normal people," Nick said out loud.

The prospect held a great deal of appeal for him. It had three years ago. It still did.

Now he was taking a vacation. That's what normal people did. Normal people flew to Florida. Normal people sat around on the beach. Normal people did nothing. That's what Nick had been doing for the past week.

It was driving him nuts.

He unlatched the gate and sauntered out of the garden. Before he knew it he was walking along the beach in the direction of the other cottage.

Miss Melina Morgan.

It was just his luck to get stuck on Simon's private island with a librarian. It was a little—a lot, in fact—like being stranded on a deserted island with a nun.

What did you say to a lady librarian? Read any good books lately?

Melina with the incredible blue eyes. What was she doing here, anyway? There had to be better places for her to vacation than on the same stretch of white sand as him.

He made a decision. He would ignore her. He would pretend that she didn't exist, that they had never met, certainly that she had never seen him naked.

A rush of undiluted, and unexpected, sexual desire shot down Nicholas Hazard's body and gathered in his groin, with the normal results.

The girl had seen him without a stitch on, and yet he was the one getting turned on. In self-disgust Nick kicked at a seashell that had washed up on the shore.

Ms. Morgan was hardly a girl by anyone's standards. She must be twenty-five if she was a day. Maybe even thirty. Not so long ago society would have labeled her a spinster, an old maid. Surely seeing a man "in the flesh" wasn't a new experience for the woman. She had to have had her share of male admirers over the years.

But another possibility niggled at him. What if she hadn't? What if a lady librarian in a small midwestern town where everybody knew everybody else's business had to live an exemplary life, a life without blemish, a life without scandal, a life without sex?

Sex.

"You're a fine one to talk." He gave a self-deprecating laugh and shook his head from side to side. "How long has it been for you, Nick-o?"

Too long.

Way too long.

He liked to think he was a man of discriminating tastes, but he had been in and out of nearly every major city on the face of the globe without forming a lasting relationship with a "normal" woman. His life-style wasn't conducive to dating a lady lawyer or a teacher or a librarian....

Caribbean blue.

Nick bit off a brief expletive. He was not interested in Melina Morgan. Melina Morgan was not his type.

What was his type?

He only knew what it *wasn't.* It *wasn't* some sweet young thing. It *wasn't* some innocent virgin. It *wasn't* a librarian from some small town in God-knew-where, Wisconsin.

On the other hand, maybe Ms. Morgan wasn't as guileless as she appeared. Maybe she was on vacation for the simple reason that it afforded her the opportunity to get away from the watchful eyes of the good citizens of Moose Creek. Maybe the lady was here for some fun in the sun.

Nick glanced up. He wasn't completely surprised to find himself standing outside the pink cottage, appropriately named since the painted pink bungalow was decorated with pink shutters, pink-trimmed windows, pink doors and even pink flowers.

There was something about Melina Morgan, something he couldn't quite put his finger on, something mysterious, something almost . . . secretive.

He'd learned a long time ago to trust his instincts when it came to situations and to people. It had served him well again and again, and it had saved his skin on more than one occasion. His instincts told him now that his guest—well, Simon's guest—was hiding something. Instead of ignoring her, he'd better keep an eye on her.

There was a light on in the cottage. Apparently the lady hadn't retired for the night. Nick reached out and opened the garden gate.

Maybe, just maybe, the lovely Ms. Morgan was here for some fun in the sun. Maybe that was her secret.

Surely he hadn't guessed her secret.

He couldn't know. There was no way he could know. His offhand comment had been just that—an offhand comment, a careless quip, a lucky guess that he didn't even realize was a lucky guess. After all, his conversation with her on the beach earlier that evening had been slightly flirtatious and more than a little outrageous. Just the kind a man like Nicholas Hazard would have with a woman. Melina imagined he was quite the ladies' man: all that blond hair, all those muscles, all that bronzed skin...

Well, she did have a secret, but she wasn't about to tell Mr. Hazard or anyone else on these islands. They wouldn't believe her, anyway.

She sat down at the mahogany desk in the library of the pink cottage. Perhaps cottage was a misnomer. The house was a spacious fifteen rooms, complete with six bedrooms, six bathrooms and all the amenities, including beautifully engraved stationery that read Cayo Hazard, The Florida Keys. There was even a discreet imprint of a peacock fanning its feathers at the top of each page, in honor of the flock of fowl that had been imported by the original owner.

At least, that was the story according to the island's caretaker, Sweet Pete, who had delivered her to Cayo Hazard in his boat.

These were the most luxurious surroundings Melina had ever seen, let alone stayed in. Indeed, she would never have agreed to Simon Hazard's suggestion that she use his beach cottage if she had known it was an island paradise.

She permitted herself a small sigh. It was too late now. She was here, and she was on a quest, a mission, the adventure of a lifetime!

Melina switched on the desk lamp, opened the carry-on bag she had hauled all the way from Wisconsin and carefully removed a small chest. It was a replica of a travel trunk, the type used by pioneers going west in Conestogas, or by young ladies of breeding journeying to the New World to join fathers and brothers and husbands.

Or by pirates who were about to bury their ill-gotten treasure of gold and silver, emeralds and diamonds.

Her heart beat faster.

Removing a chain from around her neck, Melina inserted the small ornate key dangling from the end into the miniature lock on the front of the chest.

Click.

It unlocked. She lifted the lid. Inside was a piece of foolscap yellowed with age. She carefully removed the scrap of paper and spread it out on the desk in front of her.

It was a map.

She knew it by heart. She had studied the crudely drawn map a dozen times, a hundred times, in the months since she had found it in the attic of her parents' home.

She traced the details with the tip of her finger. There was the chain of islands—she knew them to be the Florida Keys. There was a treacherous reef along with a sandbank and shallows, an island shrouded in mist, a cave and a cove. And there—there was an *X* to mark the spot!

There was also a warning: a faded skull and crossbones, and a bit of scribbling that she could barely make out in some places, and was completely illegible in others.

What she could decipher, Melina read aloud.

Look ye in the monath of ———.
Look ye high and low at ——— noon.
Look ye by the lighte of the ——— ———.
If ye wold find the ——— ———.

Down at the bottom of the page was clearly written in what appeared to be a schooled seventeenth-century hand: "A curse be upon any soul who dares to pilfer the God-given treasure belonging to Sir Henry Morgan."

A shiver coursed down Melina's spine when she read the words. It was part fear, part dread, part excitement, part eager anticipation.

Sitting up straight in her chair, she gave herself a stern lecture. "You'll never find what you're looking for, Melina, if you don't get to work."

She rummaged around in her carry-on luggage and came up with a legal pad, a pen, a handful of pencils and a map of current-day Florida. These were followed by tracing paper, a ruler and a dictionary. She spread the items out on the mahogany desktop and was quickly absorbed by her task.

First she must find the missing words of the rhyme. Then she needed to superimpose a modern map of Cayo Hazard and the surrounding islands over their historic counterparts.

Before long Melina had a lengthy list of potential clues. Absentmindedly she chewed on the end of her pencil and muttered, "Noon. June. Dune. Tune.

Rune. Soon. Loon. Coon. Moon. Moonflaw. Moonling. Moonblind. Moonward. Moonrise. Moonscape. Moonless. Moonbeam. Moonlight. Moonset. Moonquake. Mooncalf. Moonstruck." She gave a weary sigh and stretched her arms high over her head. "You've been making lists for weeks. I think you're beginning to show definite signs of being moonstruck, yourself." With that she crumpled up the sheet of scratch paper and tossed it into the wastebasket beside the desk.

She decided to study the maps.

"You've got one major problem," Melina informed herself a few minutes later. "Water."

They were all islands. There was water everywhere. And she didn't know the first thing about scuba diving, snorkeling, swimming, or operating a boat.

Nicholas Hazard was right. Under the circumstances, what in the devil was she doing on a Florida beach?

But she knew the answer to her own question. She was fulfilling her dreams.

She had dreamed of handsome pirates and swashbuckling sea captains since she was a little girl. She had imagined herself as the damsel in distress rescued by D'Artagnan and his fellow musketeers. She had been the exotic beauty in league with the mysterious Count of Monte Cristo. Indeed, she had played every role from Joan of Arc to a penniless princess.

Eventually she had given up her girlhood dreams and become a practical young woman and a respected professional in her community.

Until this spring.

April 26, to be exact.

That was the day she turned twenty-nine. That was the day Melina Morgan realized, beyond a shadow of a doubt, that there was no Prince Charming waiting for her just around the next bend in the road, no knight on a white charger, no royal duke disguised as a doorman.

She would be thirty years old on her next birthday, and life was slipping away from her without a Grand Adventure, without excitement, without mystery or intrigue or romance.

The very next week she had met Simon Hazard, and he had insisted that she make use of the cottage on Cayo Hazard. It was the beginning of her dream coming true....

Footsteps.

Melina was yanked back to the real world. She heard the sound of footsteps on the porch outside her window. The hair on the back of her neck and on her scalp stood on end. An icy-cold chill slivered down her spine. She was suddenly covered from head to toe with gooseflesh.

Very carefully and very deliberately—yet nonchalantly, she hoped—she refolded the treasure map and returned it to the miniature chest. She slipped the chest back into her carry-on, under a pair of silky underthings. Pushing the map of Florida and the legal pad of paper aside, she got to her feet. She walked across to the French doors and casually looked out.

There was no one in sight.

Melina hadn't known she was holding her breath until she exhaled.

Knock.

Knock.

Someone was at the front door. Her heart was pounding; it resounded in her ears like the roar of the surf as she scurried down the hallway. She peered through the glass panes. She could make out the shadowy outline of a man. Then he turned his head, and she saw who it was.

Melina opened the front door and stepped out into the tropical night.

Nicholas Hazard was leaning back against the porch railing, his arms folded nonchalantly across his chest. "I hope I didn't frighten you."

"You didn't," she lied.

"I wasn't sure you'd recognize me in the dark."

Melina blurted out the first thing that popped into her head. It wasn't until the words were spoken aloud that she realized how they sounded. "It wasn't the dark. I didn't recognize you with your clothes on."

Three

"That's not what I meant to say," Melina quickly retracted, the heat shooting to her face.

A lazy, masculine smile raised the corners of Nicholas Hazard's mouth. "Somehow I didn't think it was."

"Well, it was and it wasn't," she waffled.

"I quite understand."

Taking a deep breath, she decided to begin again. "What I meant to say is that you look different—"

"Dressed?"

"Yes." Melina wasn't sure what to do with her hands. She finally stuffed them into the pockets of her bathrobe.

"Most people do look different with clothes on," he teased, his chest rising and falling beneath his faded T-shirt.

"I'll have you know that I don't usually put my foot in it," she stated in her own defense.

"I assumed not."

She sniffed. "You seem to find it amusing."

"I'm afraid so."

Her eyes narrowed slightly. "And entertaining."

"Vastly."

"Perhaps even laughable."

His lips were twitching. "The word laughable has a negative connotation."

Melina lifted her chin. "Nevertheless, you are laughing *at* me, Mr. Hazard. And please don't claim that you're laughing *with* me."

"All right, I won't. But please call me Nick." After a short pause he added, "The ability to make people laugh is a gift."

She heaved a deep sigh. "Only if you mean to be funny."

He frowned. "Being funny inadvertently doesn't count?"

"Nope."

Nicholas Hazard rubbed his hand back and forth across the nape of his neck. "That's a shame. It seems to me that most of the humor in life is either accidental or incidental." Then he brightened. "If it will make you feel any better, you look different, as well."

"I do?"

"Yes."

She was almost afraid to ask. "In what way?"

"The last time I saw you—" he made a curvy gesture with his hand "—you were wearing something very sleek, very chic and very black."

The *only* time he'd ever seen her, Melina qualified.

He went on. "And I seem to recall that your swimsuit had a tendency to ride up in the, uh, rear."

The heat rushed to her face a second time. "It's the darn design. The legs are slashed to here." She indicated somewhere between her thigh and her waist.

Tawny eyes were glued to the spot. "Yes." A chiseled chin was thoughtfully stroked. "I see."

"Well, I don't see how a woman can be expected to swim in the stupid thing."

Her companion seemed to take the matter under serious consideration. "She isn't."

She made a soft "posh" sound with her mouth. "Then why call it a swimsuit?"

Broad shoulders were raised and then lowered again. "It's one of the great mysteries of life." He spoke courteously, but his gaze was shuttered. "I didn't wake you, did I?"

"No."

"I was pretty sure I saw a light on."

"You did." Melina glanced down at the chenille robe that covered her from neck to ankle. "I, uh, I was taking a bath."

He flashed her a quick grin. "I hope you stayed at the shallow end."

"Don't worry, I did." It was no joke considering the size of the tub in the cottage's master bathroom. It had roughly the dimensions of an Olympic swimming pool.

Her late-night visitor unfolded his arms and reached out to trace the monogram on her bathrobe lapel. *"M M M,"* he read aloud. "I know the Melina part and the Morgan part, but what does the third *M* stand for?"

Melina hesitated. Then, dropping her voice slightly, she confessed, "It's a closely guarded secret."

Nicholas Hazard's ears seemed to perk up. He pushed himself off the porch railing and took a step closer to her. She was very aware of his size, his strength, his interest. "Really?"

She nodded. "No one in Moose Creek even knows."

"No one?"

"No one," she assured him.

"How singular."

He was starting to make her a little nervous. She rattled on. "Well, no one besides my mother and father."

"Naturally they would know your middle name."

"Naturally."

The man seemed inordinately interested in the subject. For the life of her, Melina couldn't imagine why.

"We have to assume the doctor who delivered you knows," he suggested.

She tapped a fingernail against her bottom lip. "I assume he does."

"And the hospital employee who filled in the blanks on your birth certificate."

"I suppose so."

"The clerk at the courthouse."

She intended to put a stop to it now. "All right. I guess a few people know. But it is not common knowledge."

"What is it?"

"What is *what?*"

"What is your middle name?"

She drew in a long breath and let it out slowly. She would probably regret telling him. "*M* is for Magdalene."

For a moment or two there was no reaction or sign of recognition on the handsome face. Perhaps Nicholas Hazard wouldn't make the connection. "Wasn't she a fallen woman?"

He'd made the connection. "Yes."

His eyes glittered like gold. "Hasn't the name come to represent a reformed prostitute?"

She shouldn't have told him. "I'm sorry I told you."

"Don't be."

Self-consciously she twisted the belt of her bathrobe. "I've thought about changing it, but I'm afraid it would hurt my parents' feelings."

"Trust me," he said with a crooked smile, "nothing is as bad as my middle name."

That got her undivided attention. "Nothing?"

The handsome blonde immediately started to backtrack. "I shouldn't have mentioned it."

"It's too late now."

"I guess it is."

"Fess up," she prodded.

He blew out his breath. "In preamble, let me state that my mother is a very sweet woman. She's just a bit different."

"A bit different how?"

"For one thing, she's a poet. For another, she's a leftover hippie from the sixties."

"She sounds—"

"She is."

Melina looked up at him. "You're putting off the inevitable, Mr. Hazard."

"I'm trying my best, Ms. Morgan."

"Sooner or later you're going to have to tell me."

"I suppose so."

She wasn't about to let him off the hook. "Turnaround is fair play. I told you my middle name, and now it's your turn to tell me yours."

"You won't laugh."

"I'll try not to," she said, wetting her lips with the tip of her tongue.

"Longfellow."

Melina wasn't sure she'd heard him correctly. "I beg your pardon."

"My middle name is Longfellow," he repeated. "My full name is Nicholas Longfellow Hazard."

She promised herself that she would resist temptation, that she would keep her eyes *up* and forward.

She would not look down.

She would certainly not steal a glance at the man's crotch.

"Go ahead," he urged with a great sigh that sent the muscles of his chest rippling.

Melina swallowed hard. "Go ahead?"

"Go ahead and laugh. You have my permission. Trust me, you won't hurt my feelings," he said with another long-suffering exhalation. "There isn't one joke, one pun, one double entendre, one sexual innuendo that I haven't heard at least a hundred times, a thousand times, in the past thirty-four years."

"I know how you feel."

"You do?"

"Any librarian would."

That declaration appeared to catch him off guard. "Any librarian?"

"We hear them all."

Nick leaned back against the porch post and gazed down into her face. "For example?"

She thought about it for a minute. "Librarians do it by the book."

He coughed discreetly.

"It wouldn't have been so bad," she explained, "but a former colleague of mine had it printed on a bumper sticker. She drove the car forever, too."

"That type always does."

"Then there's the old line about assisting someone with their research."

"That is a very old line."

Melina pursed her lips in thought. "Every year, there's at least one nine- or ten-year-old boy who believes he's the first to come into the library and ask for a book by Ima Hogg or Urinal Smoothie."

"Unbelievable."

"The older boys are more blatant. They'll march right up to the front desk and inquire in a loud voice where the section on sex lives of the Arctic mosquito are located."

"Amazing."

"We all know, of course, that there are no mosquitoes within the Arctic Circle."

"How could there be? All that ice, all that snow."

"Exactly." Melina folded her arms beneath her breasts. "Yes, we librarians have seen—and heard—it all."

"Seen *and* heard?"

She looked up. Nick was watching her intently. "Stories, of course."

"Of course." There was a count of three. "What stories?" he inquired.

"Well, there's the standard tale about finding a skeleton in the storage closet."

"Did you ever find a skeleton?"

"Thankfully, no. Then there's the one about the ghost of Moose Creek's first librarian appearing in the stacks and shhing anyone who speaks too loudly."

"Go on," he urged.

Melina lowered her voice to a conspiratorial whisper. "I know for a fact that my predecessor wore rubber-soled shoes so she could sneak up on unsuspecting couples and catch them in the act."

"In the act?"

She nodded. "In flagrante delicto."

There was a flash of perfect white teeth against bronzed skin. "This gets more intriguing by the minute."

"I deliberately wear shoes that click on the library's hardwood floors, myself," Melina told him with what she hoped was a casual air. "It gives everyone fair warning. But every once in a while I'll still come across a boy and girl so engrossed in each other that they don't hear me."

"What do you do then?" he asked, obviously deeply interested.

"Back away as fast and as quietly as I can and try again, usually calling out to someone in a loud voice."

Nick appeared scandalized. "A loud voice in a library?"

"Sometimes extraordinary circumstances," Melina informed him with her usual no-nonsense attitude, "call for extraordinary measures."

"Sin in small-town America." He shook his head from side to side. "Even in Moose Creek, Wisconsin."

"Moose Creek is no different than any other place," she informed him.

Something flickered behind the tawny eyes. "Tell me about the men of Moose Creek?"

Melina drew a blank. "The men?"

"You know, the males. The opposite sex from females. The other—if not the better—half of the population."

"Why?"

"I want to know what's wrong with them."

Melina was intensely aware of Nicholas Hazard's vibrant body and its proximity to hers. "There's nothing wrong with the men of Moose Creek."

"Sure there is." He delivered the punch line. "Not one of them has had the intelligence to snap you up."

She gave a tired laugh. "That was very smooth, Mr. Hazard."

"Nick," he prompted.

"That was very smooth, Nick."

"I thought so."

"Do you usually get results with a line like that?"

He shrugged his broad shoulders. She assumed that meant he did.

What was sauce for the goose was sauce for the gander in Melina's book. "Tell me about the women of—?"

"Chicago," he said, filling in the blank for her.

"What's wrong with them?"

"Nothing."

"There must be," she echoed. "Not one of them has managed to snap you up, have they?"

"Nope." Nick shifted his considerable weight from one foot to the other, although Melina knew firsthand that he was all sinewy muscle and long, lean, masculine body. The subject of women was apparently not one he cared to discuss with her. He abruptly inquired instead, "How are you getting along in the pink cottage?"

"Fine."

"Do you have everything you need?"

"I do."

"Did Sweet Pete show you around?"

"He did."

"The housekeeper comes over from Key West three days a week. She brings in supplies, cleans the cottages, does the laundry and even a little cooking if you wish."

"So Sweet Pete said."

"Is your fridge well stocked?"

"There's enough food in it to feed an army," Melina informed him with a touch of irony.

"Fresh towels and sheets?"

"Yes."

"Bed comfortable?"

"Very."

"Air-conditioning cooling properly?"

Melina gave him a wry smile. "It's all right, Nick. You're not my keeper, and you're not my host."

"But Simon is."

"Simon isn't here."

"That's my whole point."

"Everything is fine. Everything is more than fine," Melina reassured him. "It's wonderful. In fact, it's perfect."

"Good."

She took a breath. "That still doesn't make you responsible for me."

"That is a matter of opinion."

She took another deep breath and finished firmly, "I'm a big girl, and I can take care of myself."

"All the same, if you need anything, don't hesitate to call," Nick offered.

"Call?"

"Dixie cups."

"Dixie cups?"

The man held up the index and middle fingers on his right hand. "Two, and a very long string."

Melina looked up at him as if he had taken leave of his senses.

Nick explained. "If you pick up the telephone in your bedroom, it automatically connects with one in my bedroom."

"How very cozy."

He was innocence itself as he raised both his hands in mock surrender. "Hey, it wasn't my idea. It wasn't even Simon's. The telephones were already in place when he bought the island from its previous owner."

Melina stifled a yawn. "I believe you."

"I'd better be saying good-night. You look tired."

"It's been a long day."

"You can say that again."

"It's been a long day."

He chuckled. It was a deep, rich, masculine sound that tiptoed down her spine, one vertebra at a time. "Say good-night, Melina."

"Good night, Nick."

"Good night, and welcome to Cayo Hazard." He was at the gate before he turned back and said, "Don't forget to lock up after yourself."

"I won't."

Although who was going to disturb her on an isolated island with nothing but water and more water for as far as the eye could see?

Who besides a very tall, very muscular, very blond and occasionally very naked Nicholas Hazard?

Melina locked the front door behind her and walked down the hallway to the library, shutting off the lights as she went. She suddenly realized just how exhausted she was. Her investigations would have to wait until morning. Tomorrow was, after all, another day.

She shoved the pad of paper, the handful of sharpened pencils and the map of modern Florida into the top drawer of the desk. Her hand was poised above the switch at the base of the lamp when she happened to glance down.

"That's odd," Melina muttered to herself. "I could have sworn..."

The wastebasket beside the mahogany desk was empty. The sheet of scribbling she'd been working on and then tossed into the basket early that evening had disappeared.

She shrugged. Maybe she'd missed. Maybe the wad of paper had hit the tiled floor and rolled under the massive desk or beneath a chair.

After all, who would want to break into a cottage in the dead of night to steal a worthless piece of scratch paper?

Four

The man took the piece of scratch paper from his shirt pocket. He spread it out on the table in front of him and pulled up the overstuffed chair. The once soft, buttery leather on the arms was brittle from use and age; it was cracking in several places. Like most of the furniture in the bungalow, the chair had seen better days.

He sat down and leaned forward, focusing the beam of light from the reading lamp directly onto the paper. It was a list of words, neatly written by a female hand. He glanced down the page.

Noon.

June.

Dune.

Tune.

Rune.

Soon.

Loon.

Coon.

Moon.

Baffled, the man shook his head. What was she up to? Why, at an hour well past midnight, was Ms. Melina Morgan sitting at the mahogany desk in the pink cottage scribbling a list of rhyming words?

It could be, he reflected, something as simple, something as innocent as working a crossword puzzle. But he doubted it. There was too much evidence to the contrary: the map of Florida, the tracing paper, the pen and pencils, and whatever the sneaky Ms. Morgan had quickly stashed in her carry-on luggage when she'd heard his footsteps on the porch.

It was unfortunate he hadn't remembered how sounds carried on the island at night. It was quiet. Too damned quiet, as far as he was concerned.

He reached up and fingered the fashionable gold chain around his neck. Why was Ms. Morgan here? More important, what did she mean to the Hazards?

At the mere mention of the name—he didn't give a tinker's damn if it was Simon Hazard or Nick Hazard or any other Hazard; one was as bad as another—a feral grin transformed his features from handsome to frightening.

Revenge.

All he cared about now was getting back a little of his own. Well, *a lot* of his own. He would be the first to admit he needed the money, too. He always needed money. Some people thought he was a greedy bastard. Maybe they were right.

"You bastard, where have you been?" came a shrill female voice from behind him.

His spine stiffened. He hated it when she'd been drinking. He always had. He could tell from the ironclad control she was trying to maintain over herself that she had been at it all night.

Her words were only slightly slurred. "I said, where have you been?"

He didn't bother to look up. "Out."

"Out? Out where?" She made a grand, sweeping gesture with her left hand. The large "rock" on her ring finger caught the lamplight and sparkled like a brilliant star. It wasn't real, of course. He knew for a fact that she'd hocked her real diamonds a long time ago to pay for her twin vices: bridge and brandy. This one was for show, as was so much in her life. "It's three o'clock in the morning," she announced as if he couldn't read the time.

"I had business to take care of."

She snickered. "Business?"

"On the island."

She slowly sank into the equally worn leather chair on the opposite side of the table. "You've been visiting the island?" The realization seemed to take the wind out of her sails for a moment. Then she perked up and cooed in mock maternal tones, "How are my precious ones?"

He was tempted to tell her the truth—that he hadn't seen her damnable birds—but he didn't. Not that they were *her* birds any longer. They had been sold along with everything else on the island, right down to the last stick of furniture and the shirt off his back. "The peacocks are fine."

She crossed one elegant leg over the other. "I hear there is a Hazard in residence," she said with genuine disdain.

He nodded. "Nick."

She deliberately tried to bait him. "The big, blond, good-looking one?"

He ground his teeth together. "That's the one. There's a girl, too."

She leaned forward. He could smell the brandy on her breath. "Are they sharing a cottage?"

He shook his head.

She persisted, digging for any morsel of gossip she could spread like manure at the bridge table. "Do you think they're sleeping together?"

Her eagerness repelled him. "I wouldn't know."

She glanced down, then squinted at the item he held between his hands. "What do you have there?"

"A piece of paper."

"I can see that much for myself. Where did you get it?"

"I discovered it in a wastebasket in the library of the pink cottage," he explained.

"What's written on it?"

"A list of rhyming words."

She frowned. Something she did as rarely as smiling, since either one might cause wrinkles. "What does it mean?"

"I don't know." He carefully refolded the piece of paper and returned it to his pocket. "But I intend to find out."

The woman nervously twirled the large fake stone in her hand. "I need some money," she finally blurted out.

He held his breath. "How much this time?"

She picked a spot over his left shoulder and stared at it. "Five thousand." She swallowed with great difficulty. "In cash, please."

"Five thousand!" He brought his hand down on the table with a resounding thud. "Where in the hell am I supposed to get that kind of money?"

She avoided meeting his censorious gaze as she suggested, "You could always sell one of your ponies."

She'd forgotten. He already had. Every last polo pony was gone now but Rasputin.

"Money doesn't grow on palm trees," he reminded her in a deeply sarcastic voice.

"I—I know."

"You shouldn't bet so much on bridge. You were never that good a player."

"You're right, of course, dear."

"I can manage to give you a thousand."

"I suppose it will do."

"It will have to do. I have expenses, as well, you know."

"I know."

"You've got to economize."

"I try."

Maybe she did. "Try harder." He wanted to be alone. "Go to bed now. It's late."

Unsteadily she rose to her feet. She balanced herself against the table for a moment. "What are you going to do?"

"What am I going to do?" he repeated, stroking the side of his aristocratic nose with his index finger. "I'm going to study this list, and then I'm going to keep a close watch on our guests. A very close watch."

"Clever boy," the woman murmured as she swayed toward her room at the back of the bungalow. "I always said he was a clever boy."

Five

He was up to no good.

It was the only logical explanation for Nicholas Hazard's behavior last night.

He had been gracious.

He had been charming.

He had been the perfect host.

He had, in short, been too good to be true.

Melina didn't believe for one minute that he'd had a change of heart. He did not want her on Cayo Hazard. That had been made clear from the first moment he'd walked out of the water.

Admittedly he had been at something of a disadvantage at their initial meeting. Admittedly there had been extenuating circumstances. Admittedly they had started off on the wrong foot.

"The wrong foot? Is *that* what you call it?" Melina softly chortled to herself as she collected her belongings for the trip to Key West.

She liked to think she wasn't a skeptic by nature. Indeed, she had always believed in the essential goodness and honesty of people until proven otherwise. But she was about to make an exception for the man next door.

Whether it was gut instinct, some kind of sixth sense, or plain old feminine intuition, it didn't take a Philadelphia lawyer to figure out that Nicholas Longfellow Hazard was up to something.

Perhaps he didn't trust her. Perhaps he was afraid she would abscond with the family silver or the monogrammed tea towels. Perhaps he was simply suspicious by nature. One thing was clear: he was keeping an eye on her.

"You'd make a lousy spy, Mr. Hazard," Melina muttered as she tossed a mesh shopping bag over her shoulder. "You're far too big and far too obvious."

She locked the front door of the pink cottage behind her and took off along the garden path. She was halfway to the dock when another thought suddenly occurred to her.

What if the man had ulterior motives?

"Good grief, now your imagination really is running wild," she said with a laugh.

She didn't believe for one minute that Nicholas Hazard was interested in her as a woman. She wasn't his type. He wasn't her type.

What was her type?

"Sensitive. Intelligent. Kindhearted. A man interested in books and in the pursuit of knowledge." Melina recited her wish list out loud. She wouldn't mind if he was also suave, debonair and dressed to kill.

Then why did she dream of sword-wielding pirates and swashbuckling sea captains? And why had she fallen asleep last night with Nicholas Hazard on her mind?

"Stuff and nonsense!"

She had more important things to do than argue with herself about men. She was on her way to Key West. She was determined to hire an instructor to teach her how to swim, how to snorkel, how to read the tides and how to maneuver a boat through hazardous waters. Everything she needed to know, in fact, before she could continue with her quest.

Melina stepped down into the small boat tied up at the dock and studied the dashboard. Surely any reasonably intelligent human being could figure out how to operate one of these contraptions.

She turned the key in the ignition.

Nothing.

She tried again.

Again, nothing.

Fifteen minutes later she was still trying—to no avail. By now she was hot and tired and thoroughly frustrated.

She took off her straw hat, wiped the perspiration from her forehead and plunked the hat back down on her damp hair. "Damn! And double damn!"

"Tsk, tsk," came a familiar voice from behind her. "Is that any way for a librarian to talk?"

Speaking of the devil...

Melina tried not to groan. Reluctantly she turned and raised her eyes. It was Nick. He was standing on the pier, arms folded across his chest, legs planted solidly apart, watching her every move.

"Going somewhere?" he inquired blithely.

She was up to no good.

It was written all over her lovely face. He could read the woman like an open book.

Her generous lower lip protruded slightly. "It's broken," she announced.

He could be tolerant. He had all the time in the world. "What is?"

"The boat." She was obviously thoroughly exasperated. "It won't start."

Nick stepped down into the sleek Fiberglas model, worked the controls for a minute and then turned the key. The engine sprang to life. "You have to put it into gear, like a car."

"Oh..."

"Do you know how to drive a stick shift?"

"No."

"Have you ever operated a speedboat before?"

"I'm a quick study," Melina Morgan assured him. "Why don't you show me?"

"It's a little more complex than that. Where do you want to go?"

"Key West."

Nick gave her a bright smile. "You're in luck, then."

"I am?"

"I just happen to be on my way to Key West this morning." He was willing to bet that the incredible blue eyes were mere slits behind her sunglasses.

"That's quite a coincidence," she finally said.

"Yes, it is."

Her weight was shifted from one sandaled foot to the other. "Why?"

"Why what?"

"Why are you going to Key West?"

Nick had to think fast. Then it came to him. "To buy a razor." He palmed the week's growth of beard on his chin. "I need a shave."

"I noticed."

"Why are you going to Key West?"

"Sightseeing."

Her answer sounded a little too pat to Nick, but he tried to be open-minded about it. After all, this wasn't an official interrogation. "Planning to go any place special?"

"I want to visit the historic house and gardens where John Audubon lived while painting wildlife in the Keys in the early 1830s."

"A natural choice."

"I'd like to see the Spanish-colonial villa where Ernest Hemingway wrote *For Whom the Bell Tolls* and *The Snows of Kilimanjaro.*"

"You might find the six-toed cats a curiosity."

"And the penny Hemingway threw to the ground, complaining that his wife was extravagant, and she might as well take his last cent, too."

"I see you've been boning up on the history of our little island," Nick remarked as he cast off from the pier. "Speaking of which, Cayo Hueso is the Spanish name for Key West. It means Bone Island."

"How did it get that name?"

He touched lightly upon the grisly details. "For the piles of human bones supposedly found in the mangrove clumps."

Melina shivered and wrapped her arms around herself. "I think I'll skip the mangroves."

Nick took a deep breath of salty air and gazed out over the blue-green sea. "You're a woman of imagination, Melina. Think of Key West as it must have been in Hemingway's day. Exotic. Remote. A colorful blend of Cubans and local fishermen, sailors and bootleggers. It was 1928, after all. Life was simple here. Elemental. Filled with wonderful native foods—turtle steak, conch salad, black beans and yellow rice. The houses were built of coral rock taken from the ground on which they stood, and quickly became overgrown by palms and banyans and philodendrons." Unknowingly he gave a sigh. "A man could spend his life fishing, eating, drinking—"

"And making merry?"

"Something like that."

He could *feel* Melina watching him.

"You love it here, don't you?" She seemed surprised, as if she had just made an amazing discovery.

A muscle in his face started to twitch. "I love it and I hate it."

She wanted to know more, of course. A woman always did. "Explain."

He tried. "I love the water. I love the remote islands and the virgin beaches untouched by modern man. I love the dingy old bars along the waterfront and the ramshackle shops that have sprung up like weeds by the docks. I love the shellman who brings in his nets every morning and whacks open the conchs with his machete. I love the smell of the place, the taste of it."

"And what do you hate?"

"I hate the high society. I hate the tourist traps. I hate the glitz and the glamour and the commercialism. I hate what has been lost forever, and I hate like hell the fact that I didn't get to see it."

She took it back. She took it all back: every last unflattering remark, every nasty comment—spoken aloud or not—every unkind thought.

Nicholas Hazard was not a beach bum. He was not a ne'er-do-well. He was not just another surfer, swimmer, volleyball-playing blond bimbo sporting a perfect tan and bulging biceps. He was definitely not an insensitive, bungling oaf or an overgrown male ego.

The man had the heart and soul of a poet.

No one could have been more astonished than she was, Melina realized.

"Well, here we are," Nick announced as he expertly guided the sleek boat alongside the dock.

"Thanks for the lift," she remembered to say as he helped her ashore.

"You're welcome."

She hesitated. "What time are you planning to head back to Cayo Hazard?"

"I have a few errands to run, and a razor to buy, of course." He glanced down at some kind of special watch on his wrist. "Why don't we synchronize our watches and arrange to meet back here in, say, three hours? Will that give you enough time?"

"It should."

He gave a grunt. "I'll even take you to lunch at one of my favorite places."

"I don't want to be a bother."

"You're no bother."

She wasn't convinced of that, but, under the circumstances, it would be rude to refuse. "Lunch would be nice."

"We'll meet at twelve noon, here."

"Twelve noon on the dot." Melina pointed to her feet. "Right here."

"I have precisely eight forty-eight."

Melina glanced down at her watch. It said eight-fifty. That was close enough. "I have the same."

"Where are you off to first?"

"Why do you want to know?" she heard herself blurt out.

Nick laughed and backed off. "Hey, I didn't mean to pry. I was just going to volunteer to point you in the right direction."

She was mortified. "I, uh, I think I'll start by taking in some local color."

He waved and started down the street. "Adios, then. And have fun."

Melina watched him go. Then she dug into her handbag and took out the slip of paper with the address Sweet Pete had given her yesterday.

Five minutes later she was standing in front of the business establishment recommended by the caretaker. She looked up at the weathered sign hanging over the door. The letters were faded by rain and wind, salt and sun, but they were still readable. Bloody Mary's. Scuba Diving, Snorkeling, Fishing, Live Bait, Lunch.

She double-checked the street number. This was the place. Melina tucked the address away, opened the screen door and went in.

Six

There was *stuff* everywhere.

Rods. Reels. Plastic floats. Wet suits. Flippers. Fishing tackle. Lures. Hats with built-in personal fans. Life vests. Goggles in every imaginable size and color. Waterproof watches. Swimwear. Sunglasses. Bug repellent. Shark repellent. Beach towels. Beach blankets. Beach bingo.

Boxes of stuff. Shelves of stuff. Tables of stuff. It was piled knee-high, waist-high, shoulder-high and right up to the ceiling.

Melina didn't think she had ever seen so much stuff crammed into so little space.

"Need help?"

She turned. There was a teenage girl standing behind her, snapping her gum and wearing the tiniest bikini Melina had ever set eyes on. "Y-yes."

"What are you looking for?"

"Snorkeling equipment."

A voice from the back of the store bellowed, "Chantal! Chantal, come here this instant!"

"Snorkeling gear, aisle five," Chantal said and took off.

"Aisle five," Melina repeated.

A quarter of an hour passed. She was on the verge of giving up the search when a man of indeterminate years approached her. He was wearing a cap with the slogan Fish Or Cut Bait printed in chartreuse letters across the bill. "You need some help, missy?"

"Yes, I do."

He flashed her a friendly grin. There were two prominent teeth missing from the front of his mouth. "That's what I'm here for... to help."

"I'm looking for aisle five," she told him.

The man took off his cap, scratched his head and gnawed on his bottom lip for a moment. "Don't believe we've got an aisle five."

Melina took a different tack. "Snorkeling gear?"

His face lit up. "Back wall, southwest corner," he stated and disappeared.

Melina was left standing there, her mouth agape. "Southwest corner?"

She was still trying to determine which direction was north and which was south when a woman came bustling up to her. The newcomer was tall—a good six feet—red haired and freckled. Perhaps this third time would be the charm.

"Have you been helped?" came the inquiry in a very proper British accent.

Melina wasn't certain how to answer the question. "There was a girl—"

"A tiny thing in an even tinier bikini?"

"That's the one."

The woman sighed and confessed, Melina thought rather reluctantly, "My niece."

"Chantal?"

"Chantal."

"Well, Chantal told me snorkeling gear was on aisle five, but I can't seem to locate an aisle five," she explained to the redhead.

"I can't say I realized we even had an aisle five."

"That's what the man claimed."

"The man?"

"The one in the fishing cap and with several teeth—" Melina pointed in the general direction of her mouth "—missing in the front."

"Conch."

She frowned in puzzlement. "Conch?"

"That's his name. Conch."

"How unusual."

"Conchs, pronounced konks, are descendants of the original settlers. They're native-born to the island."

"How interesting."

"I didn't even know Conch was about the place this morning." The Englishwoman brushed a short, carrot-colored wisp back from her face with one hand. "It's been a bit crazy around here. Let me introduce myself. I'm Mary Worthwyle. Better known to the locals as Bloody Mary."

"Are you *the* Bloody Mary?"

"You mean is that my name on the sign out front?"

"Yes."

"Yes." The Brit took another swipe at her unruly mop; it didn't do any good. "I imagine you're wondering how I got a nickname like Bloody Mary."

It looked as if it was going to be one of *those* days. "How did you?" asked Melina.

"Some think it's because of the popular tomato-juice-and-rum drink served with a stalk of bushy green celery." Mary Worthwyle shuddered visibly and shook her head. "Can't stomach vegetable drinks, myself. Or anything served in a pineapple with one of those cute little paper umbrellas sticking out of the top. My drink is Scotch. No soda. No water. No ice."

"Vodka," Melina corrected.

"Vodka?"

"A Bloody Mary is tomato juice and vodka."

"I'll have to remember that." The proprietress was warming up to her subject now. "A few years ago there was a rather dotty old dear who lived here in Key West. She liked to go around regaling tourists with stories about me being the English version of your American Lizzie Borden. No need to explain where the Bloody Mary would have come from in that case."

Melina felt it was an appropriate time to mention, "The term 'Bloody Mary' probably originated with your Queen Mary I of England."

"Of course," acknowledged the woman. "I should have thought of that." Her eyes grew shrewd. "You're a clever little thing."

"I'm a librarian," Melina explained.

"Books?"

"Books. But back to your nickname—"

"I'm afraid the truth isn't half as exciting as some of the wild tales you'll hear. I'm part of what the travel brochures refer to as local color."

Melina had told Nick she was going to start by taking in some local color.

"Anyway, I digress. When I first came to the States from England—it must be nearly twenty years ago now—we were vacationing at the newly opened Disney World. You know, the one in Orlando."

Melina knew.

"Anyway, I loved the place. Florida, that is, not Disney World. I took to it like a duck to water. The rest of the tour group went home after our holiday, but I didn't. I never did go back, in fact." The woman's voice trailed away as she gazed off into the distance.

"Bloody Mary..."

Her eyes focused. "Yes—"

"Your nickname," Melina prompted.

"My nickname? Oh, yes, my nickname. Then there's the school of conjecture who believe it all started with my red hair." She put a hand to her head and gave it a pat. "Not true." Her voice sank to a confidential level. "Comes from a bottle, dear. Has since 1967."

Melina was genuinely curious. "What is the truth, then?"

"I suppose it began my very first day on Key West." The Englishwoman stopped to interject, "You must remember I hailed from London. Gray skies, fog and smog, rain and more rain." She made an expressive face and continued. "Anyway, I had never been to a tropical paradise before. I recall going around exclaiming about the bloody bright sun and the bloody blue skies and the bloody white sand and the bloody beautiful water." She paused, and then concluded, "I believe that's where the bloody nickname came from."

Melina couldn't help herself. She laughed out loud. "My favorite scenario, I think, is the one where you're England's answer to Lizzie Borden."

Mary Worthwyle laughed along with her. "That just happens to be my personal favorite, as well."

Melina noticed there was something silk-screened on the front of Mary's T-shirt. But since her arms were folded across her rib cage, only the first few words were visible. Is That Your Snorkel...

She tried not to stare. "Speaking of snorkels—"

Bloody Mary dropped her arms and slapped her thigh with the palm of her hand. "That's right, you were interested in snorkeling gear, weren't you? Follow me."

As they took off down the narrow store aisle, Melina caught a glimpse of the T-shirt and the entire message emblazoned across the chest.

She nearly choked on her own saliva.

She envisioned that split second last night when Nick Hazard had walked out of the ocean without a stitch on. It played over and over in her mind's eye.

For spelled out in big bold letters across the shopkeeper's ample bosom was: Is that Your Snorkel, Or Are You Just Glad To See Me?

Mary came to a dead stop in front of a wall of shelves. They were crammed with an assortment of masks and snorkels. "Now, what do you need?"

Melina tried valiantly to collect her wits. "I, uh, I don't know."

"Do you want to rent or buy?"

"I'm not sure."

"How much do you wish to spend?"

"How much does it cost?" After all, her shopping list was long and varied.

Mary was the picture of patience. "Are you a beginner, my dear?"

"Yes, I am."

"Now we're getting somewhere," she said. "How much of a beginner are you?"

Melina was embarrassed to admit the truth. But in the end there was no way around it. "I can't even swim."

"Then how fortunate that I can," came a smooth, cultured, resonant baritone.

Both women turned. There was a man lounging against the center post in the aisle behind them. He was watching their every move.

Melina heard her own sharp intake of air. The stranger wasn't just good-looking. He was the *best*-looking man she had ever set eyes on. Indeed, from the top of his slicked-back salon-styled jet black hair down to his highly polished Gucci loafers, he was the essence of male perfection.

And he knew it.

Mary's demeanor was suddenly cool, and her accent even more pronounced. "Hello, Mr. James."

There was the merest hint of an acknowledging nod. "Hello, Mary."

"What brings you to this part of town?"

His only answer was a condescending smile.

Mary Worthwyle looked him straight in the eyes. She seemed determined not to be intimidated by the man. "Slumming today, are we?"

He studied the professionally manicured fingernails on first one hand, then the other. "*We* are shopping."

"Shopping?" she snorted.

"Actually, I came to speak to Conch about doing some odd jobs around the estate." His gaze never once left Melina. "Aren't you going to introduce me to this lovely young lady?"

"Can't."

Something flickered for an instant behind the intense, dark eyes. "Can't or won't?"

"Can't," Mary repeated. "I don't know the young lady's name, myself."

"Then we have been remiss in our duties, haven't we?" he drawled. Although what duties those could be were beyond Melina. Elbowing the older woman to one side, he grasped her hand in his and raised it to within a hairbreadth of his mouth. "I am Hunter Beauforth James the Third. To whom do I have the pleasure of... of... *ah-choo!*"

"Sneezing on?" Melina finished for him in a dry voice.

"Beautiful and a sense of humor, too." He dropped her hand and reached into the pocket of his perfectly creased trousers, emerging with a white linen handkerchief. "Slight allergy," he said, dismissing the problem.

"To work," Mary muttered under her breath.

He looked askance at the shopkeeper. "Surely you have something you need to do somewhere else."

Bloody Mary made no move to leave. Much to Melina's relief. "No, as a matter of fact, I don't. I'm helping this young lady select her snorkeling equipment."

Apparently Hunter James wasn't about to let the woman's presence deter him. He leaned toward Melina and lowered his voice to a caress. "Has anyone ever told you that your eyes are the most incredible color?"

"They're just blue," she said.

"Just blue!" His tanned, aristocratic features assumed an expression of utter disbelief. "They're not just blue. Your eyes are the color of the sea when the sky is without a solitary cloud in it and the sunlight filters down to the coral reef."

Melina wished he would go away. "That's very kind of you," she said without enthusiasm.

"Yes, it is," he responded with a flash of perfect teeth. What other kind of teeth would a man like Hunter James have? "But you still haven't told us your name."

There was no sense in being coy about it, she decided. The man was obviously capable of hanging around until she told him. And, after all, both he and Mary had already introduced themselves. "Melina Morgan."

"Where are you from, Miss Melina Morgan? It is Miss Morgan, isn't it?" He captured her hand again, making a small production of examining the ring finger for evidence of her marital status.

"I'm from Wisconsin."

"Wisconsin?" echoed Mary. "Isn't it cold there?"

"Yes."

"Doesn't it snow in Wisconsin?"

"I'm afraid so."

The transplanted Floridian shivered. "You must be here on vacation."

"I am." She dug into her handbag. "Sweet Pete gave me the name and address of your shop."

"Sweet Pete, that old reprobate!"

Hunter Beauforth James III did not like being ignored. "So you're the young woman staying on Cayo Hazard."

She looked at him. "How—?"

"It's a small world, and good news travels fast," he said by way of an explanation.

"Besides, everybody knows everybody else's business on Key West," Mary piped up.

Melina shook her head. She thought she'd left that kind of thing behind in Moose Creek.

"I'm serious about offering you my services, Miss Morgan," the handsome man stressed.

"Exactly what kind of services would those be?" snickered Bloody Mary.

Hunter James attempted to look down his aristocratic nose at the redheaded woman. No small feat, when she was every bit as tall as he was. "I heard Miss Morgan confess to you that she didn't know how to swim. I would consider it an honor and a pleasure to teach her."

"Miss Morgan won't be needing your help." All heads turned at the sound of a dark, gritty, masculine voice. "I'll teach Melina anything and everything she needs to know."

Seven

Nick didn't know the man, but he knew the type.

Slick.

Arrogant.

A snob.

A bit of a prig.

A very smooth operator when it came to women.

He'd seen the way the guy had been fawning over Melina for the past few minutes. He had watched her watching him. She wasn't as immune to his charms, his wealth, his dark good looks as she thought. She was only human.

Nick had a stern talk with himself. *What* Ms. Morgan did, and *who* Ms. Morgan did it with were none of his damned business. She was a big girl now, as she was fond of reminding him. She could take care of herself.

On second thought, maybe she couldn't. Maybe she *was* his business. He was a Hazard, after all. And she was a houseguest on Cayo Hazard.

Nick made up his mind. He had to act and he had to act fast. He told himself it was for her own good. In fact, he was doing Melina a favor. He was saving her a lot of grief in the long run. Someday she'd thank him. For, whatever her claims to the contrary, she needed a keeper.

He took a step closer and slipped an arm securely around her waist. Then he pressed her into his side and smiled down at her possessively. "*Sweetheart,* why didn't you tell me you were ready to take the plunge?"

The innuendo was clear to everyone.

Bloody Mary laughed throatily.

The smooth operator frowned.

Melina opened and closed her mouth without managing to utter a single coherent sound.

"I'm ready, willing and, I might add, able to teach you anytime, anywhere," he volunteered.

The girl tucked under his shoulder sputtered like a fish out of water. "I—you—"

"You wanted to surprise me, didn't you?" Nick said, putting words into her mouth.

He took a moment to notice that Melina had a very pretty mouth. Just the right size, just the right shape and eminently kissable. He wondered what she would taste like, feel like, how she would respond....

"You—you—"

"I know. I know. Now I've gone and ruined your surprise, *honeybunch.* But it's the thought that counts." He hoped she remembered that later when he tried to explain why he had come galloping to her rescue.

All of a sudden Nick felt his stomach muscles tighten. It was that old familiar feeling in his gut. The one he got just before things went from bad to worse.

"Haven't I seen you somewhere before?" It was more of an accusation than a question.

Nick glanced at the other man. "I doubt it."

A condescending finger was pointed at him. "Don't you work at the club?"

He went very still. "At the club?"

"The Key West Club." Dark eyes narrowed maliciously. "I recognize you now. You're one of the boys who cleans up after the ponies."

There was an audible gasp from the young woman beside him. Apparently she knew a deliberate insult when she heard one.

Nick nearly laughed in the man's face. The dark-haired Lothario was a rank amateur compared to the first-class professionals he'd come up against in his time. Somebody was always trying to get a rise out of him, to get his goat. It was one of the hazards of the job.

His half brother, Jonathan, was a living legend in the security business. And he wasn't half bad, himself. They were both known for having ice water running through their veins, and for possessing an incredible—indeed, an enviable—degree of self-control.

That's why he wasn't going to smash the guy's pretty face in.

Nick knew he appeared cool, calm and collected. "I'm afraid you've got the wrong man."

"I don't think so."

"I know so." He casually turned his head in the direction of the door. "That your sports car parked out front?"

"Yes, it is. Why? Would you like to take a closer look? She's a beauty. I'll bet you've never seen anything like her in your entire life."

Nick grunted. "Had one."

"*You* owned a Lotus?"

He managed to smile without displaying a trace of humor. "Sold it."

"Sold it?"

"It was a piece of expensive junk." He lost the smile. "You're blocking the entrance to Mary's store. You need to move your automobile."

The man grew livid. "Just who in the hell do you think you are?"

"A law-abiding citizen and a paying customer." He turned to Bloody Mary. "Have you got that special diving gear you ordered for me?"

She nodded. "Sure enough."

"I asked you a question, boy," the man snapped with self-importance.

Nick ignored him.

"I said, who in the hell are you?" A half-hearted attempt was made to grab his arm.

"I'm a tourist just like any other tourist."

"Bull."

"I'm not looking for trouble, mister. But unless you want every bone in your hand broken, you will remove it now." He meant business.

His arm was dropped like a hot potato.

"A tourist just like any other tourist." Bloody Mary seemed to find that amusing. "Don't be so modest, Nick."

"I'm on holiday," he stated emphatically. "This is the first vacation I've taken in years."

"Simon mentioned something to that effect before he left for—" Mary Worthwyle made an airy gesture with her hand "—Timbuktu."

"Simon didn't go to Timbuktu," piped up Melina. "He went to Myanmar."

"Myanmar?"

"Burma. They changed the name."

"Oh. Anyway, it's time you two gentlemen were introduced. Nicholas Hazard—" the Englishwoman looked from one to the other "—Hunter James."

It was a good thirty seconds before either spoke.

"Hazard."

"James."

"You're on vacation."

"I'm on vacation."

"You're related to Simon Hazard."

"Yup."

"Then you must be staying on his island, too."

"I am."

"I didn't realize you knew the young lady."

"Now you do."

Hunter James looked directly at Melina. "Nevertheless, my offer still stands."

"If Miss Morgan is genuinely interested in learning how to swim, snorkel, scuba dive or just about anything else there is to do with the water, she's already got the right man," Bloody Mary announced cheerfully.

"Mary—"

"This is no time for modesty, Nick. Not with you being an ex-navy SEAL, an expert diver, a champion surfer and swimmer and knowing boats inside and out the way you do."

"Nick is obviously a man of many, many talents," Melina agreed.

There was something in her voice, something Nick couldn't quite put his finger on. He might have won the battle, but he had the oddest feeling that there was a war going on, and *it* was far from over.

He was shark bait.

Dog meat.

Cattle fodder.

She was going to cut him up into tiny pieces and feed him to the fishes.

She was going to tear him limb from limb, have him drawn and quartered, make him walk the plank.

He was going to have to face the music, take his medicine, pay the piper. . . one penny at a time. After all, he had made his bed, now he must lie in it.

Bad choice of words.

The minute they were alone—Hunter James had wisely decided to take his precious car and vamoose; Mary was waiting on another customer—Melina slipped out from under Nick's arm and spun around to face him.

She was steaming. "What, pray tell, was that all about?"

He looked mildly affronted. "I think you know what it was about."

"Why don't you tell me?" she said, removing her straw hat and lifting the loose, damp hair from her neck.

"It was a pickup."

Melina drew a blank. "It was a truck?"

Nick scowled at her. "I'm not talking about that kind of pickup."

She tossed back her hair. "Oh, you mean sex."

"Yes, I mean sex. The guy was making advances."

She narrowed her eyes. "I could have sworn he was offering to teach me how to swim."

Nick appeared to smother a laugh. "You didn't believe that old line, did you?"

"Was it a line?"

"Ah, c'mon, Melina, we're both adults."

"That is debatable."

His lips tightened. "I decided I had to take matters into my own hands and stop it before it got started."

"Whatever *it* was."

Frowning, he crossed his arms. "I warned the guy off. I staked out my territory. I let him know in no uncertain terms that you were unavailable. I felt it was my duty."

Her blood pressure shot up. "Your duty!"

"My duty and my responsibility."

"Your duty and your responsibility!"

"You don't have to repeat everything I say," he told her.

"I am repeating everything you say, Mr. Hazard, because I can't believe I'm hearing it," she ranted.

Nick stepped closer. "As your host—"

"You are not my host."

"As your protector, then—"

"I do not need a protector."

"As a kind of surrogate big brother—"

She rolled her eyes. "Oh, brother, is right."

Nick plucked a snorkel off a nearby shelf and took a minute to examine the breathing apparatus. "Do you have any idea how much is charged for my professional services?"

Melina was still miffed. "Your professional services as *what?*"

He returned the snorkel to the shelf. "As a bodyguard, of course. Although, frankly, my brother, Jonathan, and I both feel that 'security consultant' is a more accurate term. It reflects the years of experience and the kind of expertise we bring to our very select clientele."

She planted her hands on her hips. "Are you trying to tell me that all that male posturing, all that peacock tail-feather fanning, all that gamesmanship and one-upmanship was supposedly for my own good?"

"Yes."

She sank her teeth into her bottom lip. "From whom were you protecting me?"

"Hunter James."

She laughed right in his handsome face. "Hunter James?"

Apparently Nick failed to see the humor. "James is a snob and a prig."

"I agree with you."

"He's a snake."

"Very likely."

"He's also a jackass."

"Well, there's no law against being a jackass. Half the men in America are guilty of that," Melina informed him.

The skin around his mouth grew even more taut. "The guy is a smooth-talking Lothario who seduces innocent young women and then leaves them without so much as an adios."

"I didn't realize you knew the man."

"I've never seen him before in my life."

"Then how—?"

"I know the type."

"The type?" she hooted.

Nick nodded. "A wolf in designer sheep's clothes."

"Good grief."

"His kind always preys on helpless women."

"I'm anything but a helpless woman."

But he wasn't listening to her. In fact, not a word she said seemed to register with Nick.

He gave another decisive nod of his head. "You wouldn't have had a chance up against a pro like James. Someday you'll thank me."

"I'll thank you to mind your own business," she muttered under her breath.

"Hunter James expects every woman he meets to fall into his clutches like an overripe plum." Nick raised his hands between them, palms up.

He glanced down.

She glanced down.

His hands were directly in front of her breasts.

He quickly dropped his arms to his sides and looked up. He cleared his throat and rambled on. "He thinks he's God's gift to women. I can't stand a man like that."

"Then you can imagine how a woman must feel." Melina tried to ignore the heat rising to her face.

Nick shuffled his feet. "Maybe I came on a little strong."

"Maybe a little."

"I didn't mean to be patronizing."

"I hope not."

"I thought you were in trouble."

It had been broad daylight. She had been in a public place, an accredited business establishment. She had been picking out snorkeling gear. The proprietress of the shop happened to be a six-foot-tall Englishwoman. How much trouble could she have been in?

Melina heaved a deep sigh. "It's rather sweet in a way, I suppose."

Nick looked at her askance. "Sweet?"

"The fact that you thought I was a damsel in distress."

"What in the hell are you talking about?"

"Sir Galahad."

"Sir whoahad?"

"Surely you've heard of Sir Galahad. He was a knight of the Round Table—pure, noble and unselfish."

"Sounds like pure hogwash to me." He rubbed his belly. "I'm hungry. Let's eat."

Melina glanced at her watch. It was half past ten. "Isn't it a little early for lunch?"

"I missed breakfast."

She'd skipped everything but a cup of coffee herself this morning. "Where are you taking me?"

"Taking you?"

"For lunch. You mentioned earlier that one of your favorite restaurants was around here."

"It is. We're there."

"Bloody Mary's?"

Nick smacked his lips. "Mary makes some of the best seafood chowder in the Keys."

Melina tried to swallow the lump that had formed in the back of her throat. "Really—"

"There's some kind of secret ingredient, but she won't tell anybody what it is."

She recalled the faded sign hanging over the front door: Scuba Diving, Snorkeling, Fishing, Live Bait, Lunch.

"It makes my mouth water just to think about a bowl of Mary's chowder," Nick said.

Melina pressed a hand to her midsection. "I think I've lost my appetite."

He seemed unconcerned. "You'll find it again."

"I don't think so."

He patted her on the shoulder as they sat at the small counter in the back of the shop. "You'd better eat up, Melina. You'll need your strength."

"For what?"

"Training."

"Training?"

"And lessons."

"Lessons?"

"I'll make out a schedule after we eat. We'll be at it from dawn to dusk."

Her voice grew faint. "Dawn to dusk."

"Work. Work. Work."

"But I'm on my vacation."

"It's a good thing, too," he observed. "It gives us more time to work on your deficiencies."

Her deficiencies! "You really were a navy SEAL, weren't you?" she said sharply.

"Five years."

"And a champion surfer?"

"In my youth."

"An expert diver?"

"Required skill for a frogman."

"Boats?"

"I once built my own from scratch."

He was, indeed, a man of many talents.

She bared her teeth. "Exactly what is it that you intend to teach me?"

"How to swim." Nick grinned at her. "I thought we'd start with a simple breaststroke and go from there."

Eight

Hazardous duty. In the military it meant a high-risk assignment requiring a soldier with nerves of steel.

Not long ago Nick had teased his older brother about taking a case involving a beautiful and intelligent Egyptologist, and a pharaoh's ransom in antiquities. It had been risky business from the start. Jonathan was now married to the brainy beauty, and they had recently returned from their honeymoon.

But Nick had never once thought that teaching a young woman how to swim could be dangerous. Of course, he had never tried to instruct Melina Morgan.

On the surface she appeared to be a fairly pretty, mild-mannered, rather staid librarian from a small midwestern town. Instead, she was living proof of the adage *Never judge a book by its cover.*

For underneath it all she was a woman of fiery passions, of surprising strength, of rare sensuality. She was one of the fabled mermaids of old seen by lonely sailors on long journeys across the seven seas. She was a temptress, a siren of ancient Greek mythology enticing him with her bewitching sweetness and songs, luring him to his ultimate destruction.

"You're off your rocker, Nick," he muttered under his breath as he watched his star pupil attempting to float on her back several feet from him.

Melina was a dead weight in the water. She started to slowly sink to the bottom. He reached out and cupped her derriere—her lovely derriere—in the palm of his hand.

"Head back!" he barked. "Chin up! Spine arched! And, remember, stay relaxed!"

She was as stiff as a board. Her eyes were squeezed tightly shut. Her teeth were leaving marks in her lips. Her hands were clenched into fists.

"At ease," he growled.

"Wh-what did you say?" Melina gulped, taking in a mouthful of brine as she flailed her arms and tried to stand in the waist-deep water.

He caught her about the middle and dragged her up beside him. "I said, at ease, Ms. Morgan."

She coughed once or twice and pushed the strands of wet hair away from her face. "How am I doing?" she asked, looking up with a hopeful expression.

The situation called for diplomacy. "You're making progress every day."

She didn't just smile; she beamed at him. "Do you really think so?"

Nick chose not to give a direct answer to her question. "If you could only learn to enjoy the water."

"How can I enjoy the water when it positively scares me to death?" she pointed out.

He pondered the problem. "What we need to do is replace your fear with a feeling of pleasure," he said, thinking aloud.

"Pleasure?"

"You trust me, don't you, Melina?"

There was only the slightest hesitation on her part. "Yes, I trust you, Nick."

"Then go along with me on this, okay?"

"Okay."

He had an idea. It just might work. "I'm going to lie back in the water. I want you to stretch out alongside me."

"Alongside you?"

He nodded and continued explaining his plan. "I'm going to wrap my arm around you. You rest your head on my shoulder and swing your leg over mine." It was a brilliant scheme. "We'll float together."

She didn't argue with him. "Whatever you say. You're the teacher."

Yes, he was. So hands off, Hazard, he reminded himself for at least the twentieth time that day and the umpteenth time that week. This was strictly business!

He lay back in the tropical waters and turned toward the warmth of the sun. There was so much joy to be had in the sea, so much relaxation, so much pleasure. To think that Melina was missing it all.

His determination grew stronger. He wouldn't give up. He would help her. He would teach her. Or, by God, he'd know the reason why!

Sliding an arm firmly but gently around her waist, he lodged her against his body. They were side by side, bare skin to bare skin, except for the scraps of colorful material that made up her swimsuit and his abbreviated trunks.

She nestled her head in the crook of his arm. He could feel the silky strands of her hair floating around them. One stray wisp caught on his lip. He touched it with the tip of his tongue. Her hair tasted of salt water, smelled of the sand and the sun and faintly of coconuts. The latter must be from her shampoo.

She hooked her leg over his and they floated together on the surface of the blue sea.

"I want you to relax, Melina," he murmured in hypnotic tones. "I have you now. I won't let anything happen to you. I'm right here."

Nick kept up the litany until he felt her body release its tension and her breathing slow. He turned his head. Melina's face was raised to the sky. Her eyelashes had fluttered shut. She appeared to be sound asleep. It was the first time he had seen her in the water unafraid.

He took the opportunity to study her features. They were delicately drawn, from the arch of her brows to the point of her determined chin. Her skin was pale, but flawless. There was a tiny mole just behind her ear.

Nick suddenly had the craziest urge to kiss her behind that ear.

He watched the natural rise and fall of her chest as she breathed in and out. He imagined what she would look like bobbing on the surface of the ocean, her hair encircling her head like a dark wreath, her breasts bared to the elements, their rosy tips breaking free of the water.

He could see himself bending over her and licking the salty essence from her nipples, nibbling on the tender peaks, watching them curl up like delectable sea urchins. He would strip the swimsuit from her body. He would study the small pool that formed in her belly button. He would envy the ocean that washed up between her thighs, the little waves that broke against that most feminine shore.

Up periscope!

If he wasn't careful he was going to embarrass himself, Nick realized.

He stood. "That's enough for today."

Melina's eyes flew open. She dropped her feet to the cushion of sand on the ocean floor and jumped up and down for joy. "I did it, Nick! I floated!"

"Yup."

"I didn't sink to the bottom like a dead weight."

"Nope."

"It was wonderful."

"I told you it would be."

She reached out, grabbed his hand and urged him toward her. "Can we do it again?"

He dragged his feet. "Now?"

"Why not?"

He couldn't blurt out the truth. He couldn't admit that he had become sexually aroused by the thought of her naked body floating on the surface of the water.

"Why not?" he echoed.

"We usually work later than this."

"We do."

"There's still plenty of daylight left."

"There is."

"It's too early to eat dinner."

"Although I seem to have worked up quite an appetite," he confessed.

She gave him a funny look. "Are you hungry?"

A groan escaped him before he could stop it.

Melina moved closer. The water lapped around her slender form. "Nick, are you all right?"

"Sure."

"You don't look all right to me."

He didn't feel all right, either. But there wasn't much to be done about it.

Her eyes widened with concern. "Maybe you got too much sun."

Too much sun? That was rich.

Melina put her hand to his forehead. Her fingertips were cool and gentle to the touch. "I don't think you have a fever."

"I wish I did."

Her brow creased. "You do?"

"Maybe then you'd leave your hand where it is."

Something seemed to change in her voice, in her expression, as if she were aware for the first time of the sensual currents ebbing and flowing between them.

"Would you like that?" she asked huskily.

Why not tell the truth? "Very much."

She soothed his brow, then traced an imaginary line down the bridge of his nose, around the curve of his mouth and along the jut of his jaw. "You've got a nice face, Nicholas Hazard."

"Nice?"

Her hand was trembling slightly. "Nice probably isn't the right word for such a strong face, such an interesting face, such a noble face."

"There's nothing wrong with nice," he said gently.

Her eyes were dead level with his chest. She glanced up at him through smoky lashes. It wasn't done to be coy or flirtatious, Nick realized. She was simply nervous.

"I'm not very good at this kind of thing," Melina confessed, running her tongue along her bottom lip.

"At what kind of thing?"

She sighed. "At the kind of thing that's supposed to happen between a man and a woman."

"Meaning—?"

"Clever repartee. Bantering back and forth. Flirting. Dating. Kissing. Making out. Petting." Her voice grew strained. "Not to mention whatever comes after that."

"What are you trying to tell me, Melina?"

"I want to kiss you. . . ."

Nick heard the hesitation in her voice. "But?"

"But I'm not very accomplished at it."

He frowned. "You make it sound like playing the violin or the piano."

"It's not so very different."

"It isn't?"

She shook her head, and strands of jet black hair clung to her shoulders. "Kissing is a learned skill. It takes practice. Some people are naturally better at it than others. Some will never be any good at all no matter how hard they try."

"I see your point."

"What I'm trying to tell you, Nick, is that I'm not very good at kissing, but I think I could be."

"In other words, you have potential."

Her whole face brightened. "Exactly."

"I'm relieved we have that settled," he said with a perfectly straight face.

"So am I."

He closed his eyes, puckered up and waited. Nothing happened. He opened his eyes again. "Is there anything else?"

Melina swallowed hard. "I thought you might help me get started."

"I have a better idea."

She knitted her brows. "You do?"

"Why don't I start by kissing you? Once we get the hang of it, you can kiss me."

Before she could change her mind, before he could debate the wisdom—or folly—of his actions, Nick bent his head and kissed her.

The instant his mouth touched hers, Melina knew she was in over her head.

Nick kissed the way he did everything: deftly, expertly, single-mindedly and with passion.

She was a mere beginner; he was already a master. She didn't know up from down, in from out; he was in complete control of the situation and himself.

It wasn't fair.

And she would have told him so, but she was suddenly caught up against his chest, her feet dangling in the water, her hands grasping at his shoulders.

His taste was of the sea: tangy, salty, a little pungent. His skin was slick to the touch. His hair was like wet silk. He was wild and warm and wonderful.

He muttered something against her lips.

Melina drew back a fraction of an inch. "Hmm?"

"It's not true," he mumbled, finding a particularly sensitive spot behind her ear.

"What isn't?"

"You kiss beautifully," he said, and let it go at that.

She was vaguely aware of being carried toward the shore. Somewhere in the back of her mind it registered that they were stretched out on the beach and the hot sand was against her back. For a moment she saw the sun overhead and the palm trees swaying in the tropical breeze. She heard the roar of the surf against distant rocks, and the screech of a sea gull. She felt the water lapping at her toes. Then she was aware of, knew, saw, heard, felt only one thing: Nick.

There was much that could be learned from books. Melina had read books all of her life. She had devoured them. She had lost herself in them, immersed herself in people and places she would never know, never see.

Books had brought her pleasure and pain, abundant joy and great sorrow. She had laughed and cried, loved and hated—all within the safe confines of make-believe worlds.

But Melina learned more in those few minutes on the beach with Nick than she ever had from her books. She learned what it was to have a man want her, desire her, need her. She learned about passion and pleasure, sensuality and hunger of a different sort altogether.

She discovered she was a creature of the senses. She loved to smell, taste, touch, see and hear. The world was rich with textures that she hadn't noticed before: the stubble of beard on a man's chin, the sinewy muscles beneath his skin, the silky hair on his arms, on his chest, arrowing down his torso.

She was fascinated by the rainbow of color in his eyes—tiger gold and sea green, sandy brown, yellow, even flecks of blue. She was enthralled by his lips, the shape of his ears, his Adam's apple, the size and strength of his hands.

She loved to say his name. "Nick—"

She loved the way he repeated hers over and over again. "Melina. Melina. Melina."

Then he eased the straps of her swimsuit down her arms and she felt his hot breath on her skin, sensed his delight with what he had uncovered, gasped with surprise, with pleasure, when he took her into his mouth and licked the seawater from her breasts.

"Nick, my head's spinning."

"So is mine."

She put some small distance between them. "I'm frightened."

"You should be." He readjusted the top of her suit and rested his forehead against hers, blowing out his breath. "It's been a long time for me."

"For me, too." Forever.

"My self-control is apparently nonexistent. I can't seem to keep my hands off you," he admitted.

She wanted to reassure him, to tell him that it was all right, that she liked having his hands on her. In fact, she loved it.

He rolled off her and muttered in a hard, dry voice, "If you had any damned sense at all, Melina, you'd pick yourself up from this beach and run like hell."

And so she did.

Nine

She couldn't sleep.

Melina sat up in the king-size canopy bed, switched on the lamp and reached for the top book on the pile stacked beside her. She opened to the page marked and began to read.

> Sir Henry Morgan was, perhaps, the most famous of the British buccaneers who plundered ships and ports in the Caribbean during the 1660s and 1670s. He was a bold and able commander, and while duly licensed to attack his country's enemies, the Spanish considered him a pirate.

But it wasn't Sir Henry Morgan she had on her

mind. It was Nicholas Hazard. She had been tossing and turning for the past several hours, unable to forget the way he had kissed her, caressed her, aroused her.

"Damn! And double damn!" Melina muttered. She flipped to another page and continued reading.

The Spanish galleon *Nuestra Señora de Atocha* sank in a hurricane on the way back to Europe from South America in 1622. Its motherlode was scattered across virtually miles of ocean floor. Deep-sea explorers have recently brought up 170,000 silver coins, 1000 silver bars weighing between seventy and one hundred pounds each, 215 gold bars, 3000 emeralds and 500 feet of gold chain.

The amazing thing was she hadn't felt awkward or undesirable or uncomfortable this afternoon on the beach, Melina realized. In fact, kissing Nick, touching Nick and being kissed and touched by him had seemed like the most natural thing in the world.

It felt right.

Maybe it was right.

She heaved a heavy sigh, put the first book down and absently picked up a second.

Treasure hunter Mel Fisher has verified that a silver box was retrieved from the *Nuestra Señora de Atocha* with several pieces of jewelry inside. The first is an emerald-and-gold cross on a gold chain. The second is a one-stone, 15-carat emerald ring. It is speculated that such a stone could be worth $20,000 to $80,000 per carat.

Maybe it *wasn't* right.

Maybe it had simply been all that bright yellow sun, all that crystal-clear sky, all that pristine white sand. Maybe it had been the tropical breezes, the palm trees or the intoxicating scent of exotic flowers.

After all, this was Nick's first vacation in years. He had admitted as much on several occasions. And she was staying in an enchanted cottage, living a life of luxury such as she had never known before. It wasn't real for either of them.

Face it, they had been thrown together in unusual and extenuating circumstances.

He was a man.

She was a woman.

Something was bound to happen sooner or later.

"Baloney!" Melina muttered impatiently and slammed the book shut.

Thinking about what had occurred between Nick and herself, analyzing it, looking at it rationally, examining it from every angle was getting her nowhere.

She picked up an article clipped from a newspaper several months before and reviewed the story.

Folklore tells us of the bloody pirate tradition of using a recent recruit to bury the captain's treasure. Little did the new man suspect that once his back was turned, the others planned to cut off his head and dump his body in with the treasure, so his ghost would stand guard.

Melina felt goose bumps rise on her scalp, her arms, her legs. She shivered and pulled the bedcovers up under her chin. All of a sudden she was aware of being in a huge house by herself, on a nearly deserted island, in the dead of night, without another welcoming light within sight.

"Don't be a silly goose. Just because you have a vivid imagination doesn't mean you should allow it to get the better of you."

She took her pen and pad and began to jot down notes from her reading.

Research.

She was doing necessary research.

It wouldn't be long now before she was ready to continue with her quest. Nick was an excellent teacher, and she was learning quickly. She could steer a boat. She had some idea of how to determine high tide and low tide. She could swim . . . almost.

She scanned another article, paying particular attention to one paragraph.

Over three centuries later, no one knows what riches may lay buried in a cave here or a cove there, locked in the grip of a subterranean vault. Speculation centers on pirate treasure—booty left by Captain Kidd, Blackbeard, or Henry

Morgan. Others claim it is Inca gold, stashed by Spanish conquistadors. Still others believe it is bullion from the California gold rush now worth more than one billion dollars, or a king's ransom in precious stones: emeralds, rubies and priceless diamonds.

Treasure.

There were always those who would search for treasure, whether it was buried beneath shifting desert sands, the currents of the ocean, deep within the bowels of majestic mountains, or in the concealed caves of a tropical island.

Treasure.

There was always a lost thing, a lost time, a lost place, cut off from the rest of the world. Legendary cities of gold. Ancient cities hewn from solid stone. Cities beneath the sea. Cities underneath cities. Cities long ago engulfed by fire and flood, wind and earthquake, feast and famine. The quest for the lost held a fascination for some people.

People like her.

Treasure.

It filled her daydreams and her night dreams. It brought her the romance, adventure and intrigue that were missing from her life.

Melina slipped out of bed and padded barefoot to the closet where she had stowed her carry-on luggage. She carefully removed the miniature chest and unlocked the lid. She took the map and crawled back under the covers. It was time she got down to the serious business of solving the puzzle created by the illegible words.

She smoothed out the piece of foolscap and studied the faded writing.

Look ye in the monath of ———.
Look ye high and low at ——— noon.
Look ye by the lighte of the ——— ———.
If ye wold find the ——— ———.

"Look ye in the monath of *blank,*" she said out loud, toying with her pencil.

She would assume that the pirate's verse rhymed. If it was true—and at least it was a place to start—then the missing word of the first line would rhyme with *noon.* There was only one logical choice, of course. *June.*

"Look ye in the monath of June."

Melina's eyes went to the calendar clock on the bedside table. It was the first week of June. That much was no accident. She had suspected from the beginning that her search must take place in the summer.

The second line was more difficult. She began to fill in the possibilities that occurred to her. "Look ye high and low at *after* noon, *high* noon, *midday* noon, *summer's* noon, *fore* noon, *darkening* noon, *beggar's* noon...." Melina paused and pondered that one. "Or is it beggar's moon?"

This was getting her nowhere.

It was giving her an appetite, however. Or perhaps she was hungry because she had pushed the food around on her plate at dinner.

There was a telltale rumble in her stomach. She wasn't hungry. She was starved!

It seemed almost indecent when she was fretting over a man. Surely her appetite was supposed to be the first thing to go when a woman fell in love.

Fell in love?

She wasn't in love. She didn't love Nick. She couldn't. It was impossible.

A schoolgirl's crush, that was possible. A summer romance, that was possible. Infatuation, that was possible. There were all kinds of possibilities. The list was endless. But falling in love with Nicholas Hazard, being in love with Nicholas Hazard, was *not* one of them. Hunger was obviously wreaking havoc with her emotional stability.

Melina tucked the map between two pages of a book and slipped it under her pillow for safekeeping. Then she bounced out of bed and proceeded down the hallway in her bare feet. She seemed to recall a plate of cold cuts being left by the housekeeper that afternoon.

Ham and cheese on rye with a slather of mustard, that's what she needed to put her mind at rest.

She didn't bother to turn the lights on, but headed straight toward the large kitchen at the back of the cottage. That's when she heard it.

Thunk.

Thunk. Thunk.

Melina froze in place, her hand on the door of the refrigerator.

It came again.

Thunk. Thunk.

It was a muffled sound. A kind of dull thud. Man-made, she was certain of it.

She didn't dare take a breath, or release the air trapped in her lungs. The fine hairs along the back of her neck were standing straight up on end. Her heart was beating at a furious pace; it was pounding in her ears.

She couldn't move.

She couldn't speak.

Like icy fingers walking up and down her spine, the realization hit her.

Someone was in the house.

She tried to swallow and found she couldn't. Her throat was parched and desert dry. The bottom dropped out of her stomach. Her knees were jelly. For the first time in her life she was genuinely, truly afraid.

Who had said, "The only thing I am afraid of is fear?"

Was it the duke of Wellington? Was this her Waterloo?

She might be afraid, she might be shaking in her shoes—well, her bare feet—but her instinct for self-preservation was as strong as anyone's. She wasn't about to give up without a fight.

Melina quickly looked around for a weapon. Where was a nice heavy fireplace poker when she needed one? Or a sturdy umbrella? Or a baseball bat?

Her eyes lighted upon a foot-high mahogany-and-granite pepper mill on the kitchen counter. At least it was something. She grabbed the pepper mill in her hand and began to brandish it in front of her like a club.

So this was it; this was unprepared courage. "Two o'clock in the morning courage," as Napoléon called it.

Thunk.

Thunk. Thunk.

This time the sound came from the opposite end of the pink cottage.

Dear God, were there *two* of them?

She might have been brave enough to face one intruder with a pepper mill in hand, but this was a different matter altogether. This called for a strategic withdrawal.

Noiselessly Melina backed out of the kitchen and down the hallway toward the master bedroom. Ten feet from the door she turned and made a run for it.

She closed the bedroom door and flipped the lock. Then she collapsed against the cool wood. Her hands were like ice. She was trembling from head to toe.

Hysteria bubbled up in the back of her throat.

This was no time for histrionics. She had to think.

There were only two other people who belonged on this island: Sweet Pete in the caretaker's cottage and

Nick in the blue cottage down the beach. Neither of them would be sneaking about in the dead of night.

Then who was?

Bits and pieces of memories—tiny flashbacks—came to her of her first night on Cayo Hazard. She had answered the front door. She had stepped outside to speak with Nick. When she'd returned to the study, the scratch paper she'd been scribbling on and had tossed in the wastebasket was no longer there.

She had never found the wad of paper. She'd assumed the housekeeper had swept it up the next day while she was cleaning.

What if someone had been in the house that night? What if that same someone was in the house now? What if they had come back and brought along their partner in crime?

Two against one.

She needed help.

If you need anything, don't hesitate to call, Nick had said to her that night.

Call? she'd replied.

Dixie cups.

Dixie cups?

If you pick up the telephone in your bedroom, it automatically connects with one in my bedroom.

Nick.

Melina raced across the room toward the telephone. Her hand was on the receiver when she heard a scratching like a fingernail—or a claw—on glass. She glanced up.

It was a face.

It was grotesque, twisted, horrific, frightening... like a Halloween mask, and it was pressed against the windowpane of her bedroom!

She opened her mouth. No sound came out. She wanted to scream but knew she would not. Indeed, could not.

Her heart was slamming against her ribs as she grabbed the telephone that connected to the one in Nick's bedroom. It rang once, twice, three times.

An eternity later the receiver was picked up on the other end. A sleepy masculine voice mumbled, "Hello...?"

She swallowed hard. "Nick?"

"Melina, is that you?"

"Nick, come quick!"

Ten

He ran all the way.

He didn't even stop to put his shoes on, although, recalling the first night they'd met on the beach, he did slip into a pair of blue jeans.

His heart was pounding—not from the physical exertion; it was a mere walk in the park—but from fear. He was afraid. He was afraid something had happened to Melina.

The myriad possibilities flashed through Nick's mind.

She was lying on the floor in a pool of bright red blood, a knife clutched in her hand.

She was standing on a chair, quivering from head to toe, wielding a broom at a terrorized mouse or a big, black spider or a rainbow-colored snake that was native to this part of Florida. Perfectly harmless if you knew anything about snakes.

Did Melina know anything about snakes? Somehow he didn't think so.

Maybe she was sick.

Maybe she'd had a nightmare.

Maybe she'd decided to pick up where they had left off this afternoon during her swimming lesson.

"Right, Nick," he scoffed, his bare feet digging into the soft sand, his heels spraying the fine, white granules behind him as he flew along the beach.

Or maybe something, or *someone,* had spooked her, frightened her.

How much could he tell from three simple words—*Nick, come quick?*

He had to trust his instincts. And his instincts told him Melina had been scared out of her wits.

Years of conditioning kicked in. He stopped thinking and acting like an ordinary man and began to operate like the highly trained security expert he was.

He stopped a short distance from the cottage and studied the layout of the land. There were thick flowering shrubs by the front porch. They could provide cover for friend or foe. The only light appeared to be coming from the north side of the house where he knew the master bedroom was located. The upstairs was dark. The palm trees and the garden at the rear were similar to those surrounding the blue cottage.

Thankfully he wasn't going in blind. He'd had to occasionally in the past, back in the days when he was a navy SEAL, but he didn't like it.

Made him nervous.

Made his trigger finger itchy.

Gave him the willies.

Yup, surprises were among Nick's *least* favorite things.

He moved quickly, stealthily from one shadow to the next, making no sound, leaving no trace. Circling the house, he double-checked for evidence of human or animal intruders on the perimeter. He found what he was looking for by the French door outside the library.

Footprints.

He was careful not to disturb the two distinctly different sets. One was a man's boot. Large. Probably a size twelve. The other was a man's shoe of average size, no distinguishing characteristics. He couldn't tell more than that in the dark. With any luck, they would still be there in the morning.

Nick continued around to the back of the pink cottage and eased up to the windows. He peered in. No movement. No sign of life.

The kitchen door was next. He turned the knob. The door opened. It shouldn't have, of course. The house was supposed to be locked up tight as a drum.

He dropped to one knee. The lock didn't look forced. There was no splintered wood, no evidence of being jimmied. He stored that piece of information away in his brain. Either Melina had forgotten to lock the back door before retiring for the night, or someone had had a key.

Noiselessly Nick slipped into the kitchen. Then he stood in the darkness, cocked his head to one side and listened.

Outside, he could detect the gentle swish, swish of the wind as it stirred the treetops, the distinctive cadence of the cicadas and the crickets, the occasional lilting song of a night bird, the steady rhythm of the waves washing up onto the beach.

Inside, he could hear the hum of the refrigerator motor, the usual creaks and groans of any house, but no footsteps, no voices, no unusual noises.

He slid along the wall and down the hallway toward the master bedroom. Since the floor plan of the two cottages was identical, it made his job a whole lot easier.

His mind was crystal clear. His body was poised for action. His reflexes were honed to react within a split second. All of his senses were on red alert. He could see, hear, smell, taste, *sense* even the slightest change in his surroundings.

It was the damnedest thing.

He used to wonder about it. Now he simply accepted the fact that he was different, that he would always be different, that he would never be like a normal person, despite what his older brother, Jonathan, assured him.

Nick could see a light under the door of the master bedroom. He put his ear to the wooden panel. No voices. No sounds. No screams. He only hoped and prayed that he wouldn't open the door and find Melina's slender body lying on the floor hurt . . . or worse.

If anyone had dared to harm as much as one hair on her sweet head, he would track the son of a bitch to the ends of the earth or all the way to hell itself if necessary.

Nick took in a slow, steady, silent breath of air and let it out again. Then he wrapped his fist around the brass doorknob and turned it. An imperceptible push followed, but nothing happened. The bedroom door, at least, was locked.

Now he had a decision to make. Did he knock like any civilized human being? Or did he kick the bloody thing down?

Nick raised his hand and tapped lightly with two knuckles. In a calm, quiet voice that was just loud enough to be heard, he murmured, "Melina?"

There was a squeak—it sounded like a bedspring—and the pad of bare feet on tile floor. Then he heard someone say his name. "Nick?"

"Melina, is that you?"

"Nick, is that you?"

"For crying out loud, we can't stay here all night asking each other questions and nobody answering," he griped, leaning against the door frame.

The lock clicked. The knob turned. The door was thrown wide open. Melina was standing there, clasping a lethal-looking pepper mill in her hand. Her hair was flying around her face and shoulders in a dark frenzy. Her nightgown was sticking to her damp body like a second skin. Her eyes were huge and round as saucers.

Right before his eyes, her expression changed from fear to relief. She covered the last two or three feet between them and hurled herself into his arms.

He caught her.

"Nick." There was one, great, long exhalation.

He held her.

In that fraction of a second before she had thrown herself at him, it had registered in his brain that she wasn't covered with blood, that she didn't seem to have sustained any injuries or broken bones, that there were no unsightly scrapes or scratches, no nasty bruises.

Nevertheless, Nick could hear her heart pounding, feel her body trembling and her lungs gasping for air.

For at least three or four minutes, possibly longer, neither of them uttered a word. He kept her within the confines of his embrace and sent a quick prayer of thanks heavenward.

He wondered why his own heart was beating so furiously, and why he was so relieved that Melina was unharmed. It was nothing personal, he told himself.

Right, Nick-o!

Who was he trying to kid? It had been nothing *but* personal since the first moment he'd set eyes on the woman. It was about time he accepted that fact. The same way he had learned to accept the fact that he would never be normal. Why would falling in love be any different for him?

Was he falling in love with Melina?

He was very attracted to her. He'd had her on his mind right from the start. She interested him in ways no woman had in a long time. But love...

Nick's musings came to an end as he glanced up and gave the room a once-over. From his vantage point, nothing seemed out of the ordinary. There was a stack of books on the table and more books spread out on the mattress. He shrugged. The woman was a librarian. They were a breed apart. Maybe they preferred to even sleep with the darn things.

"You okay?"

"I will be," came a muffled voice, "as soon as you stop crushing my ribs."

That was when Nick realized he was squeezing her tightly, as if he would never let her go. He eased up, but only a little. "Is that better?"

Melina put her head back and gazed up at him. Tears were clinging precariously to her eyelashes. "Much."

"Are you hurt?"

"No."

"I got here as fast as I could."

Her chin quivered. "I know. But it seemed like forever."

He gazed intently into her eyes. "I've been outside for the past five minutes looking things over."

"Did you find anything?" she asked in a low, earnest voice.

"Footprints."

"How many were there?"

"Two sets. Both men."

"I thought there might be." Her lips compressed. "Do you think they're gone?"

"Chances are they're long gone."

"But they might not be."

"But they might not be. That's why I'm going to make a quick inspection of the house. I want you to stay here."

"I'd rather go with you."

"It would be more expedient if you didn't." He saw that she understood. He would be better off on his own in case there was any trouble. "I'll bring you a brandy."

"It's a deal."

"Lock the door behind me." Nick paused and dropped a swift, hard kiss on her mouth. "I'll be back."

She'd never been so glad to see someone in her entire life! When Nick had come through the door of the master bedroom her heart had soared.

When he came back Melina was nearly as relieved and as happy to see him as before. "All gone?"

Nick gave her a thumbs-up sign. "All gone. I've double-checked the doors and windows, and added a couple of security measures of my own," he said, handing her a snifter of amber liquor. "Drink up. It'll calm your nerves."

"What about your nerves?"

"I never drink on the job."

"You're on the job?"

"Not in the usual sense of the word, but I want to be fully alert tonight."

Her mouth went dry despite the liquid she had just swallowed. "Do you think they'll come back?"

"I doubt it."

"Still, you're not certain."

"They say only two things are for certain."

"Death and taxes," Melina finished for him, and took another sip of brandy. It burned all the way down, but once it settled in her stomach she could feel a warming sensation. It was quite pleasant, really.

Nick pulled up one of the chintz-covered chairs. "Why don't you sit and tell me exactly what happened?"

She plopped into the chair and took another swallow of brandy first. "This is very good," she said, studying the glass of liquor.

"It should be," Nick said with a wry smile that disappeared as quickly as it had appeared.

"Expensive?"

"Very."

"How much?"

"You don't want to know."

"In that case, ignorance is bliss?"

"Yes."

"Where was I?"

His mouth twisted. "You were about to tell me what happened here tonight."

"This morning," she corrected with a glance at the clock. "It's a quarter to three."

"What happened this morning?"

"It began an hour ago," Melina related. "I couldn't sleep, so I was reading."

She watched as Nick sauntered over to the bed and picked up one of the books. He read the title aloud. *"Pirate or Privateer—The Life and Times of Sir Henry Morgan."* He looked up with an arched brow.

"Fascinating book. You should read it sometime."

He put it down and selected another volume. *"Treasure Hunting Made Easy."*

"I saw it advertised on television. It was on one of those infomercials. The key to successful treasure hunting, according to the author of the book, is having the right kind of metal detector at your disposal."

"Which the author no doubt sells for the bargain-basement price of $29.95."

"More like $99.95." Melina made an airy gesture with her hand. "I was too smart to fall for it, of course."

"Of course." Nick examined the next book on the stack. *"Pirates and the Tradition of Sodomy in the Seventeenth Century."* He cleared his throat. "Interesting bedtime reading even for a librarian."

"Research," she stated, and took another drink of brandy. It was nearly gone. She held out her glass. "I don't suppose I could have a bit more."

"Nope. You only get enough to calm your nerves. I need you conscious."

Melina sniffed and decided to pick up her story in the middle. "Anyway, I was reading when I suddenly realized around two o'clock how hungry I was." She added in an aside, "I didn't eat much at dinner."

There was something in Nick's demeanor when he confessed, "Neither did I."

"I was on my way to the kitchen—"

He interrupted her. "Did you turn any lights on?"

"No."

"Hmm..."

"Hmm, what?"

"Go on."

"Where was I?"

"You were on your way to the kitchen," he prompted.

"When I heard a noise."

"What kind of noise?"

Melina polished off the last drop of brandy and pointed her finger at him. "I knew you were going to ask that."

"You're very astute."

"Thunk."

"Thunk?"

"That was the noise I heard. Thunk. Three thunks, in fact, to begin with," she said.

"Do you think they were natural sounds or man-made?"

"Man-made, definitely."

"Inside or outside?"

"Inside."

"Front or back of the house?"

"First the back. Then the front."

"Two intruders."

"That was my conclusion." She was quite proud of herself now that she was no longer afraid.

"Is that when you grabbed the pepper mill?"

She nodded and realized she was still holding the pepper mill in her left hand. "I would have preferred a fireplace poker or a baseball bat, but I had to improvise. I was in the kitchen. It was sitting there on the counter." She lifted her shoulders.

"Ingenious. Very quick thinking." Nick held out his hand. "I'll take that now."

"Thank you." She chewed on her bottom lip. It was slightly numb. "When I realized there were two of them I dashed back here to my bedroom. One intruder I could have handled, but I didn't care for the odds."

Nick was suddenly glaring at her with a disapproving look on his handsome face. "You actually think you could have handled an intruder?"

"Probably." She counted to three. "Possibly."

"What if he'd had a gun? What if he'd held a black belt in the martial arts and his hands were registered as lethal weapons? What if he was six-four, two hundred and twenty pounds?"

She skirted the entire issue. "As I was saying, I ran back here, locked the door, decided to call you. That's when I saw it."

"Saw it?"

Melina shuddered. "The face at the window. It was awful. It was horrific. It was a gargoyle."

"A gargoyle?"

"You know, one of those ugly statues you sometimes see on an old church."

"I know what a gargoyle is."

She went on. "I wanted to scream but I couldn't."

"That's when you said to me, 'Nick, come quick.'"

"In a nutshell, yes. The gargoyle disappeared, and I waited here for you."

Nick took the empty brandy snifter from her grasp and went down on his haunches in front of her. He put one hand on each arm of the chair and stared straight into her eyes. "Melina, it's time we had a serious talk."

"It is?"

"Yes. I've had the impression from the first night you arrived on Cayo Hazard that you've been keeping something from me."

She cautioned herself to be discreet. "What would I be keeping from you?"

"If I knew that I wouldn't have to ask you, would I?" Nick said in a reasonable tone.

He had a point. "I suppose not."

"Do you have a secret?"

She swallowed hard. He knew! He knew she had a secret. "A secret?"

"Something you're not telling me."

"I know what a secret is," she replied haughtily. What kind of idiot did he take her for?

He put a hand against her cheek. His touch was gentle and reassuring. "I only want to help you, Melina."

"I know."

"You're going to have to be completely honest with me," he admonished her.

Melina blinked once, twice, three times in rapid succession. She was acutely aware of his proximity. "Completely honest with you?"

"Do you trust me enough to tell me your secret?"

She thought about it for a minute. Then she looked into his tawny gold eyes, and she knew the answer to his question and several of her own, as well. "Yes."

His mouth turned up at the corners. "Good."

She took a deep breath and let it out again. "I'm a direct descendant, you know."

"Of whom?"

"I'll get to that." She wet her lips with the tip of her tongue. "I know where it's hidden."

Nick studied her without any change in his facial expression. "Where *what* is hidden?"

She took the plunge. "I know the location of the long-lost treasure of Sir Henry Morgan."

Eleven

"You want the rest of this sandwich?"

"I couldn't manage another bite," Melina assured him, patting her midsection. "You go ahead and finish it."

Nick wolfed down his third ham and cheese on rye with a generous slather of mustard. Then she watched him polish off his umpteenth glass of milk.

She indicated his empty plate. "Do you always—?"

"Eat so much?"

"Well . . . yes."

"Yes."

"You must have cost your parents a fortune in groceries while you were growing up."

"My older brother, Jonathan, and I consumed four gallons of milk a week." There was a flash of white teeth. "Each."

"That is amazing."

"Not as amazing as finding out that you could be the direct descendant of a seventeenth-century British buccaneer." Nick pushed his chair back and carried their dirty dishes to the sink. He ran hot water over the plates and squirted dish soap into the glasses. "I've never heard of a long-lost treasure associated with Sir Henry Morgan."

"That goes to show you how lost it really is," she said with composure.

"How many years do you think the miniature chest had been in your family's attic?"

Melina burrowed down in her chenille bathrobe and stretched her legs out under the kitchen table. "The house was originally built by my great-great-grandfather as a wedding gift for my great-great-grandmother. Each successive generation brought in their own furniture and knickknacks. Anything they didn't want got carried up to the third floor. There's stuff in the attic from before the war."

Nick casually tossed over his shoulder. "The Second World War?"

"The Civil War."

That brought him around, despite the fact he was in dishwater to his elbows. "The War Between the States? The North and the South?"

Melina nodded. "1861 to 1865." She noticed there were a few soapy bubbles splashed up on Nick's bare chest. She watched until they disappeared, leaving his skin and hair glistening.

"And nobody had bothered to examine the map until you found it a few months ago?"

"My parents were aware of its existence. They just didn't seem to care." She sighed. "Mom and Dad aren't what you would call the adventurous sort."

Nick wiped his hands on a flowered tea towel, hung it neatly over the sink to dry and leaned back against the kitchen counter. "You will discover, Melina, that there are two types of people in this world."

She gave him her full attention. "And they are—?"

"Those who dare to go in search of buried pirate treasure, and those who only dream of it."

Sitting up straight, she clasped her hands together in her lap. "Does that mean what I think it means?"

"Yup."

"Are you going to help me?"

"Yup."

"We'll split everything fifty-fifty," she offered enthusiastically.

"Half of nothing is nothing," Nick observed. "Let's not count our chickens before they hatch."

She felt it was only fair to warn him. "There's just one itsy-bitsy problem."

Tawny eyes narrowed slightly. "What's that?"

"I don't know the *exact* location of Sir Henry Morgan's buried treasure."

"You said you knew."

"Well, I do and I don't."

Frowning, Nick crossed his arms. "Maybe you should start again from the beginning."

"In that case, it would be easier if we adjourned to the master bedroom."

His raised brows rose even higher. "If you insist, sweetheart."

"It's not what you think."

"I was afraid that's what you were going to say," he muttered.

"I want to show you the original treasure map and some notes I've jotted down."

"I was hoping you were making a pass at me," he confessed, turning off the lights.

Melina knew even less about making passes at men than she did about kissing them. Not that she blamed the male population of Moose Creek—what little there was of it.

It was her. It always had been her. People said she was too picky. Maybe she was. After all, until recently she'd been waiting for Prince Charming.

Melina ran ahead and retrieved the piece of foolscap from under her pillow. She spread it out on the bedroom floor along with her scribblings, a map of present-day Florida, several notepads and pencils, and an assortment of books and newspapers she had accumulated in her research.

Nick walked around the display, stopping to read an article here, pausing to study a map there. When he came to the original hand-drawn chart he said, "I recognize this island."

Her spirits soared. "You do?"

He went down on his haunches and took a closer look. "It's called Pequeño, and it's not more than twenty nautical miles from Cayo Hazard."

Melina wondered aloud, "*Pequeño* means small in Spanish, doesn't it?"

He agreed that it did. "The island's full name translates to Small Bone Island. The original settlers to the Florida Keys thought the place was haunted and refused to go anywhere near it. The island has remained uninhabited to this day."

Suddenly Melina went cold inside. She wrapped her arms around herself. "Maybe it has something to do with the stories I've been reading."

Nick straightened. "What stories?"

"About pirates cutting off a new recruit's head and dumping his head and body in with the treasure so his ghost would stand guard."

He put a hand under her chin. "You don't believe in ghosts, do you?"

"Don't be silly. Of course not," she stated flatly. "And I don't believe in curses, either."

"Curses?"

She recited from memory, "'A curse be upon any soul who dares to pilfer the God-given treasure belonging to Sir Henry Morgan.'"

"Now she tells me," Nick teased.

Melina sniffed. "Sir Henry was protecting his assets in the only way he knew how."

"I wonder what happened to him."

"The king named him lieutenant governor of Jamaica, where he lived until his death in 1688. We assume he buried his God-given treasure prior to that time."

Nick looked at her out of the corner of his eye. "You're full of it, aren't you?"

"Full of *what?*"

"Information."

"I'm a librarian. Information is our business." She twisted the belt of her bathrobe around and around her finger. "You don't believe in curses, do you?"

"Nope."

"Well, neither do I," she reiterated.

With that matter settled, they returned to the business of buried treasure.

"Pinpointing which island is only the first step," Nick said. "We could spend a lifetime in futile search if we don't have more to go on than that."

"What about the *X?*"

He held the original map up to the light. "Could be," he murmured. "Could be."

"Could be what?"

"A cave."

"I knew that."

"Or a cove."

"I knew that, too."

"We won't know for sure until we reach the island."

Unsteadily Melina's heart began to pick up speed. "When do we leave?" She glanced at the clock. "If we go to bed now we can still get a couple hours of sleep before morning. We could set sail and reach Pequeño by noon."

Nick stopped her with a restraining hand on her arm. "Whoa! Not so fast!"

"You're right. We need a complete night's rest. And food. And water. And the proper clothes." She began to tick the items off on her fingers.

"First we have to solve the puzzle."

She snapped her fingers together. "The missing words."

"The missing words."

She plunked herself down on the floor and picked up the list of clues she'd been working on. "I'm certain I have the beginning right."

Nick peered over her shoulder. "I agree."

"The second line could be a number of things."

"High noon. Forenoon. Blue noon."

Melina stopped him. "What's a blue noon?"

He explained as he lowered himself to sit beside her. "On some of these islands you'll get a fog that appears to be almost blue-gray in color. It's usually the thickest at noon, probably due to the humidity and the trade winds. Hence the term *blue noon.*"

She read aloud, "'Look ye in the monath of June. Look ye high and low at blue noon.'" She shrugged. "Whoever wrote it wasn't much of a poet."

Nick glanced at his watch. "Hmm—"

Melina stifled a yawn behind her hand. "I guess it is late."

"Not late. Early. But that isn't what caught my interest. I was checking on the date of the next full moon."

Melina's jaw dropped. "That's it! You've done it, Nick. You've supplied the missing words in the third line. 'Look ye by the lighte of the full moon.'"

He was obviously pleased with himself. "Anyone with a rudimentary knowledge of boats could have done the same. We sailors have always steered by the stars, set our course by the rising and setting sun, the phases of the moon. There was no reason your pirate should be any different."

"That only leaves one more line."

"The last is the hardest, too. Why don't we sleep on it and try again in the morning?"

"It is morning," she reminded him, stifling a yawn behind her sleeve.

"Then we'll try again *later* this morning, after we've had some shut-eye."

"Good idea."

He got to his feet and held out his hand. "I'm going to rummage around for an extra blanket and pillow."

"Why?"

"After what happened here last night, I'm not leaving you alone."

Melina had to admit it was a relief to know he was staying. "Where are you going to sleep?"

"I'll bed down over there on the floor." He pointed to a spot where both the door and the windows were visible.

"You're planning to sleep on the tile floor?" The man was crazy.

"Believe me, I've bunked in worse places. There was one time in Moscow—"

She stifled another yawn.

"I'll tell you about Moscow another time," he said.

Melina went through the ritual of tucking the foolscap map into the small chest and locking it with her key. Then she stowed it in her closet.

She turned and glanced at the king-size bed. There was more than enough room for two people. Surely they could be adults about this. "It's ridiculous for you to sleep on the floor. We'll share the bed."

"We'll split it fifty-fifty," he proposed.

"It's a deal."

"You sleep under the covers, and I'll stretch out on top. For propriety's sake."

"There's no one here but the two of us, Nick."

"That's another reason." Then he suggested, "Why don't you crawl into bed? I'm going down the hall and take a shower. I'll be back in less than five minutes."

"Promise?"

"Promise."

Melina curled up under the covers and listened as the shower was turned on. She could picture Nick slipping out of his blue jeans. She doubted if he was wearing anything under them. There hadn't been time, after all.

She thought of that first night on the island. Nick had walked out of the sea, bestriding the world like an ancient god. Neptune. Poseidon. Adonis. Hercules. Yet he was a man, all man, a magnificent man.

What would it be like to love and to be loved by Nicholas Hazard?

What would it be like to share her bed with him? To know him intimately, as intimately as a man and a woman could know each other?

Contemplating the prospect did strange and wonderful things to Melina's insides. She was all aquiver. Something in her stomach began to flutter nervously. Her bones melted. She found herself licking her lips.

The bedroom door opened.

She pretended to be asleep. She did not want Nick to see the interest, the curiosity, the desire that must be clearly evident in her eyes.

The mattress gave way as he sat on the edge of the bed. He plumped his pillow. He ran a towel through his damp hair and then dropped it to the floor. At last he stretched out alongside her.

Melina could *feel* him watching her. She willed her breathing to remain slow and steady and regular. Still, she wasn't sure she fooled him.

Then she felt his lips gently brush back and forth across hers.

"Sweet dreams," came the husky whisper.

It was another five minutes before she had the nerve to open her eyes even a slit. Enough light entered the master bedroom from the window—the moon must be nearly full—that she could see quite clearly. Nick had a pillow bunched up at his back. One arm was tucked behind his head; the other was resting on his chest. His eyes were closed.

Her mouth and lips were suddenly dry. She tried to swallow and found she couldn't. Her heart was pounding. Surely he must hear it. It was beating *boom, da-boom, boom, da-boom.*

Nick opened his eyes and turned his head. He reached out, grasped a strand of her hair and wound it around his hand. Then he gently combed through the tangles with his fingers. "I thought you were sleepy."

"So did I."

"Aren't you now?"

"No. I can't sleep," she admitted frankly.

"Why's that?"

"I'm not used to this."

Nick rolled over onto his side. "Neither am I."

"I sleep alone."

His eyes stared hard. "I do, too."

Maybe it was the unprecedented intimacy of sharing a bed with him. Maybe it was the unusual and climactic events of the evening. But before she could censor her thoughts, Melina burst out with, "You're not my type, Nick."

He did not appear in the least offended.

"I know. And you're not mine." Then he inquired, "What is your type, Melina?"

She gave herself ample time to come up with an answer. She didn't have one. "I don't know."

"How old are you?"

"Twenty-nine. And you?"

"Thirty-four."

She was genuinely curious. "I wonder when a man or a woman figures out what his or her type is."

"Maybe it isn't a type. Maybe it's one special woman or one special man," he proposed.

"Do you really believe that?"

"I'd like to."

"So would I." There was a countable silence. "What if you wait and wait and you never seem to find that special person?"

"Then you do one of two things. You either settle for second best," he said, "or you go on waiting."

Melina wrinkled up her nose. "I don't like either of those choices."

"Neither do I."

Cool shadows enveloped her. "Do you think we recognize the other half of ourselves?"

"You mean right from the start?"

She nodded her head.

"I think we have to trust our instincts," Nick stated.

"Could it begin with mere physical attraction?" she mused, half-aloud.

"Certainly."

"With something as simple as passion?"

"It has been my experience that passion is never simple," Nick said with a sardonic smile. Then he drew in a long breath and let it out slowly. "Do you analyze everything?"

"Pretty much."

"Do you always talk so much?" he murmured at her shoulder.

"It depends."

"On what?"

"The occasion."

"I see." Maybe he did see.

"I'm very nervous."

"I know."

"I've never—" Melina swallowed hard.

"I surmised as much."

"When?"

"On the beach this afternoon."

"Yesterday afternoon," she corrected. "Did I do something wrong?"

"Nope." Nick seemed quite adamant about it. "As a matter of fact, you did everything right."

"What gave me away, then?"

He gave it about thirty seconds of thought before replying, "You aren't much of an actress."

"I assume you mean that as a compliment."

"I do." He lightly traced the outline of her collarbone. Then he went on to the shell of her ear, the little mole just behind it, the sensitive cord at the side of her neck. "You were—you are—very sweet, very genuine, very passionate."

"And very inexperienced."

"Experience is highly overrated." Nick took her hand in his and intertwined their fingers. "My instincts are usually pretty good."

After a pause she inhaled deeply and whispered, "What are they telling you now?"

"That you could be the special woman in my life," he said, squeezing her hand.

She sucked in her breath. "Nick—"

"If you don't feel the same way, tell me up front. I'm not interested in being a one-night stand."

Melina smiled tremulously. "Isn't that my line?"

"*Your* line?"

"The woman's line."

"This is the nineties. We don't have men's lines and women's lines anymore. Men and women are the same. Well, they are and they aren't."

"Make up your mind. Which one is it?" she teased.

"In some ways men and women are very different. In other ways they're surprisingly similar. The key is figuring out which is which."

"Do you analyze everything?"

"Not everything."

"Do you always talk so much?"

"Only when I'm nervous."

"Are you nervous?"

"Yes."

Melina found herself overwhelmed by curiosity. "Why?"

"You make me nervous."

She laughed. "*I* make you nervous?"

He hooked his finger under the strap of her nightgown and fiddled with the material. "You never answered my question."

"What was your question?"

"Is this a one-night stand?"

"No."

"Is it the moonlit night? Is it the tropical breezes and the scent of exotic flowers? Is it the seductive freedom of a summer vacation?"

Melina's face momentarily darkened. "I don't know." She tentatively touched his cheek, his mouth, his chin, his Adam's apple, his neck, his broad shoulders, his muscular chest. "I'd like to find out."

"So would I."

Her pulse began to beat double. "It's like going on a treasure hunt."

A smile spread across Nick's face. "I wonder what we'll discover."

She threaded her fingers through his hair; it was soft and rich and golden. "Fine silks from the East."

He dropped a delicate kiss on her mouth. "Red rubies from Thailand." His fingers brushed against her breast. "I believe I may even have uncovered a rare pearl."

He told himself to take it nice and easy. She was new at this, after all. But his body refused to listen to his brain. Once he'd touched his lips to hers, once he'd taken her into his arms, he knew where it was going to lead. He was going to make love to Miss Melina Morgan: completely, thoroughly, enthusiastically and with every ounce of passion he possessed.

The bottom line was he wanted this woman. No other would do. Only this one. It was her taste—he couldn't seem to get enough of it—the satiny feel of her skin, the fragrance that clung to her hair, the trusting way she looked up into his eyes, the intelligence and the innocence he knew was operating in that complex brain of hers. He was quite sure she had read books that he'd never even heard of. It was an enticing thought. A smart man chose a smart woman.

He suddenly wanted to make her forget anyone else there may have been. He wanted to be the center of her universe, and make her the center of his. His imprint on her would be so strong that she would never think of kissing, touching, caressing or making love with any other man.

It was a selfish thought, Nick realized.

He *was* selfish when it came to Melina. She was going to be his and no one else's. He wasn't about to share her with another man. What he took, he kept. He realized for the first time in his life how possessive he could feel about a woman, and how protective.

He was going to make Melina his—heart, body and soul.

With that little matter settled, Nick let his instincts take over. His mouth found hers, his tongue plumbed the depths. He sought the treasure he knew was there: her sweet taste, her exciting pink tongue, the little gasp of surprise as he drove his tongue into her mouth, the way she arched her body into his, wanting more, seeking more, suspecting there was so much more to come.

"Feel the way I slid between those sweet lips of yours," he muttered against her mouth.

He showed her exactly what he meant. The allusion was not lost on a woman of Melina's instinctive intelligence. She knew it was a symbolic act of what was to come.

He kissed her mouth, her eyes, the end of her delicate nose, the sensitive spot behind her ear marked by one tiny delectable mole—it always made her shiver—the tips of her fingers, her nape, the small hollow at the base of her throat, the swell of her breasts.

Her breasts were the perfect size. He took their measure with his hands and his fingers, with his tongue and his mouth. And when he drew her deeper and deeper into his mouth, rolling the tip of his tongue around the nipple, nibbling, tugging on her sensitive flesh, he heard the litany begin.

"Nick. Nick. Nick."

"Are you all right?"

"I don't know."

"Did I hurt you?"

"No. But I can't stand it."

"Of course you can."

"It's too intense."

"Lovemaking is intense."

"It feels so good."

He knew what she meant. It felt so good it was scary. "I know. I know," he groaned as her hands found his chest, as her fingertips skimmed across his nipples. They were surprisingly sensitive to her touch. He couldn't remember that happening before—anytime, anywhere.

Then her hands went to the waistband of his jeans and Nick nearly lost it right then and there.

He sucked in his breath and she slipped one hand between the denim material and his body until she reached that vulnerable flesh. He gasped.

Her eyes were dark and clouded with passion as she stared up into his face. "Did I do something I shouldn't have?"

He held on tight to his control. "No."

"Are you sure?"

"I'm sure."

"You look unhappy."

"I'm not. I am very happy."

"You don't look happy."

"Trust me, I am. It's just—"

"What?"

"That feels so damn good, honey."

She appeared relieved. "I'm glad."

Glad? He was on the verge of losing control of himself over the woman, and she was glad. Ms. Morgan was going to pay for that remark.

He kissed her until he knew her head was spinning. His certainly was. He stripped the jeans from his body and let her see, feel, experience the impact of his nudity. She seemed to find every little—and big—thing about him fascinating and worthy of further study. Then he eased the nightgown down her arms and over her hips and gave it a flick with his wrist. He thought he saw it land on a chair.

"You are beautiful," he told her.

"Do you really think so?"

"I know so."

"So are you," she murmured, rubbing her face against his chest, inhaling the distinctive scent of his body, her body, their lovemaking.

"I want to make love to you, Melina."

"I thought that's what you were doing."

"I want to go all the way."

"So do I."

"Are you sure? There's still time to change your mind." He hoped she wouldn't, but he wanted her to want him as much, more, than he wanted her.

"I don't want to change my mind. I've waited my whole life for this, for you," she said sweetly.

Nick took care of the necessities—there was no reason to be dumb about an important moment like this—and then eased her legs apart.

He kissed her again in that intimation of lovemaking and found her with his fingers. She was wet, slick, ready. He eased one finger inside her body and felt the reaction—she gripped him tightly. He knew it would be the same when he drove his manhood into her, and he groaned with need.

"Nick, I need you."

"And I need you."

"Then come here. Please."

"I'm coming, sweetheart," he promised as he drove into her body.

He heard *Melina, Melina, Melina* repeated over and over again. He never knew if it was only in his mind . . . or if he was chanting her name out loud.

Then Nick felt it begin and he shouted, "I'm coming, sweetheart."

And he did, indeed.

Twelve

What did a woman say to a man the morning after?

Actually it was the *afternoon* after, and late afternoon, at that. It was approaching evening when Melina opened her eyes, stretched her arms and encountered a brick wall beside her. It was a man's chest.

Without turning her head on the pillow she studied what she could see: a nicely shaped foot with long, straight toes; a muscular leg, tanned golden-brown by the sun; the taut muscles of a bare chest and abdomen.

Nick was covered from thigh to waist by the bedsheet. Melina didn't know if she was relieved or disappointed. She could make out the outline of his body. The parts that pushed up against the white percale, anyway.

She couldn't recall being so interested in the male anatomy before. Or, at least, certain strategic parts of the male anatomy. She had to admit she was curious, intrigued, fascinated.

She'd always known that a man was a paradox. She hadn't realized it extended to his physical body. He was strong, yet vulnerable. He was hard and soft. He was different, and he was the same.

Truthfully nothing she had ever read, or done, or thought, or even dreamed of had prepared her for the reality of making love with a man like Nicholas Hazard. It was beyond her wildest dreams.

She had changed—been changed—in a matter of minutes. She now shared a secret that women had been sharing generation after generation: when a man and a woman made love it transcended the sexual act. It rose to another level of intimacy altogether. For the world went away, and for a time there was nothing and there was no one but the two of them.

She was in love.

There was no use in denying it or in pretending otherwise. She was in love with Nicholas Hazard—completely, utterly, wholeheartedly, wildly and crazily. She only hoped and prayed that, before it was all said and done, he wouldn't break her heart.

Melina turned her head. Her eyes went to Nick's face. She found him watching her. There was no sense in being coy about it. She knew this man as she had known no other. And he knew her. He knew all about her.

A faint color rose in her cheeks. "Good morning."

"Good morning." His voice was deeper than usual.

"I guess it's afternoon."

"Good afternoon, then."

"Did you sleep well?" she inquired courteously.

"Like a baby. How about you?"

She wrinkled her brow. "I must have. I don't seem to remember a thing after the last time we..."

"Made love?"

She nodded. They had found each other again and again. The sun had been high overhead before they had fallen into an exhausted sleep.

Nick searched her eyes. "Are you getting shy on me?"

"Perhaps a little," she admitted.

He frowned in concern. "Any regrets?"

"No. No regrets. Not a one," she quickly assured him.

It was true. She had no regrets. It had been the best night of her life. Well, the best morning...

For the first time Nick smiled. "That's my Melina." He opened his arms and she went into them. She slipped into a niche that seemed made for her. "You see, you belong right there," he told her. "You fit perfectly."

"So do you," she said with a sigh, thinking of something else entirely.

She could feel her breasts skim along the ridged muscles of his chest. Her legs were intertwined with his. She pointed the big toe on her right foot and rubbed it up and down his shin. He half turned and she was very aware of his manhood, already hard, pressing against her thigh.

Nick dropped a soft kiss on her shoulder and murmured, "Are you sore?"

The soreness was inconsequential and to be expected. "A bit," she replied.

"Are you stiff?"

Melina couldn't help herself. She laughed—the hair on his chest was tickling her nose, anyway. It was a wonderfully intimate sound. "Isn't that my line?"

Nick joined her in laughter. "Maybe it is."

She twirled a small strand of his chest hair around her finger. "There!"

He glanced down as it unraveled. "What's that? Or what *was* that?"

"A French knot."

"Never heard of it."

"I'm not surprised."

His eyes were blazing. "Is it anything like a French kiss?"

"It's nothing like a French kiss."

He sighed. "Too bad."

"I was taught how to make French knots when I was a girl," she told him.

Nick sounded almost savage when he demanded to know, "By whom?"

"My mother." She could feel him relax. "It's an embroidery stitch."

"I knew that," he claimed.

She propped herself up on his chest and glanced at the bedside clock. "It's almost time for dinner."

That got his attention. "Seems like hours ago that we had our sandwiches and milk, doesn't it?"

Melina nodded. "We slept right through breakfast and lunch. Well, maybe we weren't actually sleeping at the time...." She decided to quit while she was ahead.

Nick reached over and picked up his watch from the table. He studied it for a moment. "Tomorrow night is the full moon. You know what that means, don't you?"

She made a stab at it. "You turn into a werewolf?"

"Very funny, Ms. Morgan."

"It means we need to solve the last piece of the puzzle today."

"And pack our supplies," he said.

"And get some food and clothes together."

Nick gave her a playful swat on her derriere as she slipped out of bed. "The first time I saw you I said to myself, 'Nick, the girl is cheeky, very cheeky.'"

"As I recall," Melina teased as she tied the belt of her bathrobe securely around her waist, "the same could be said for the first time *I* saw *you*, Mr. Hazard."

* * *

Look ye in the monath of June.
Look ye high and low at blue noon.
Look ye by the lighte of the full moon.
If ye wold find the ——— ———.

"My guess is whatever else we do once we reach Pequeño, we'll have to look for the *blank blank* at two different times of day," Nick speculated.

"Once at blue noon and once by the light of the full moon," Melina stated.

"Exactly." He paced back and forth across the floor of the library. "*X* marks the spot," he repeated for the umpteenth time that evening.

"*X* marks the spot," she echoed.

"*X* marks the damned spot." Nick stopped and glared at the map on the desk. "What does *X* have to do with it?"

"Everything."

"What is *X?*"

They'd been doing it all evening: using each other as a sounding board.

Melina tapped the pencil against the edge of the mahogany desk. "What is *X?*" She shrugged and answered him literally. "The twenty-fourth letter of the English alphabet."

"True."

"The Roman numeral for ten."

"True again."

"An unknown quantity in math."

"Hmm—"

She gave it one last shot. "Something shaped like an *X* or marked with an *X*."

Nick held up his hand to stop her. "Hold it. I've almost got it."

She had the sense to stay silent.

He snapped his fingers three times in quick succession. "*X* marks the spot. *X* has always been the symbol used by pirates, right?"

"Right." Melina studied the verse in front of her. "'If ye wold find the pirate's symbol'?"

"Not symbol."

"It has to be a word that rhymes with June, noon and moon," she murmured.

Nick racked his brain. "Pirate's *blank*."

Melina began to run through the list she had compiled long ago. "Noon. June. Dune. Tune. Rune. Soon. Loon. Coon. Moon."

They said it in unison. "Rune!"

"What is a rune?" Nick asked rhetorically. "It's a symbol."

"Of course, that has to be it," Melina agreed, clapping her hands together. She quickly flipped through the dictionary. "It comes from the Old Norse and the Old English word *rūn*, meaning mystery."

Nick read the reconstructed verse aloud.

Look ye in the monath of June.
Look ye high and low at blue noon.
Look ye by the lighte of the full moon.
If ye wold find the pirate's rune.

"We've done it!" Melina pushed her chair back and began to dance a jig around him. "We've done it, Nick!"

He caught her up in his arms, lifted her straight off the floor and planted a hard, swift, celebratory kiss on her mouth. "We make quite a team, sweetheart."

"I'm so excited. I don't think I'll be able to sleep a wink tonight," she confessed.

"I know a sure cure for insomnia," he volunteered.

Melina knew he was up to no good. She could see it in his eyes. But she had learned a thing or two in the past twenty-four hours. One was that it was sometimes smart to play dumb. She batted her lashes at him. "You do?"

"Yes, I do."

"What is it?"

"Rather than just *tell* you about it," Nick drawled as he carried her out of the library and down the hallway toward the master bedroom, "I think I'll *show* you."

"Oh, goody!" Melina exclaimed. "Show and tell."

What did a man say to a woman the morning after?

Actually it was the crack of dawn, barely morning at all, when Nick opened his eyes, stretched his arms and encountered a soft wall beside him. It was a woman's breast.

Without turning his head on the pillow he studied what he could see: a slender ankle, a shapely calf and leg, the taut muscles of her waist and abdomen, the delectable sight of one bare breast with its pink rosebud center.

He licked his lips, recalling the taste of her flesh, the way she responded to him without reservation, without artifice, only with passion, only with sincerity, only with her heart and soul and body.

"It's what you wanted, isn't it, Nick-o?" he whispered to himself. "You wanted her to forget any other man, every other man."

Melina was covered from thigh to waist and across to one shoulder by the bedsheet. Nick didn't know if he was relieved or disappointed. He could make out the outline of her body. The parts that pushed up against the white material, anyway.

He had always been interested in the female anatomy. What healthy heterosexual male wasn't? But there were women, and then there were women. Each one was different. Some were as different as night and day.

The female breast was a perfect example. First, they came in all sizes and shapes. Some were perky and stood at attention. Others were weighed down and tended to droop. Nipples were the same. They could be inverted or protruding. Some were pale pink, some were rosy, some were ruby red.

Melina's breasts were perfect.

He didn't think he would ever tire of looking at them, touching them, caressing them, kissing them, licking them, rolling his tongue around the nipple, drawing her into his mouth and suckling like a baby....

He had to stop or he'd drive himself crazy, Nick realized. Truthfully nothing he had ever seen, or done, or thought, or even dreamed of had prepared him for the reality of making love with a woman like Melina Morgan. She was beyond his wildest dreams.

He had changed—been changed—in a matter of minutes. He now knew what men had been discovering generation after generation: when the right man and the right woman made love it transcended the sexual act. It rose to another level of intimacy altogether. For the world went away, and for a time there was nothing and there was no one but the two of them.

Was he in love?

There was no use in denying his feelings for her or in pretending that he didn't enjoy making love to Melina. He did. He couldn't seem to get his fill of her. He took her, and an hour later he wanted her again.

Hell, he'd make love to her constantly if he were capable of it.

Nick turned his head. His eyes dropped to Melina's face. She was watching him watch her. Her lips were slightly pursed. Her eyes were midnight blue. He wondered what she was thinking about.

"What are you thinking about?" she murmured.

He had no intentions of telling her the specifics. "You."

"That was very slick, Mr. Hazard."

"Thank you. I think."

Her eyes were sparkling now. "This is it, Nick. This is the big day. I can scarcely believe it."

"Me, either."

"Are you excited?" she asked.

He was definitely excited, but he didn't think they were speaking of the same kind of excitement. "Of course I am," he answered.

"This is what I've been waiting for my whole life," she confessed to him. "This is my Grand Adventure."

Nick only hoped that the adventure—and the man—lived up to her expectations.

Thirteen

"Land-ho!"

"Land-ho?"

"I've always wanted to say that." Melina looked up at the well-worn cap Nick was wearing. Something was printed across the front. It was in a language that she didn't read, didn't understand, didn't even recognize. "Is that the latest in yachting gear, captain?"

"Captain?"

She shrugged. "Well, you're driving the ship, and you're in charge." According to him.

"This is a boat," Nick informed her. "A plain old boat. It's not a ship, and it's not a bloody yacht."

Melina pushed the hat back on her head an inch and stuck her thumbs in the life jacket strapped snugly about her body. "I'll bet Hunter James the Third has a yacht."

Nick gave a snort. "From what I found out in town this morning, Hunter James the Third probably doesn't even own an oar outright."

"Financial difficulties?"

"Try broke."

"The poor man," she sympathized. It was nothing personal, of course.

"Don't feel too sorry for him. The 'poor man' is down to his last polo pony."

"What about the fancy car?"

"Repossessed."

Melina unhooked her thumbs and pulled her hat down to shield her eyes from the sun. "It's probably better this way. You said the car was a piece of expensive junk."

"It is. It was."

She sensed Nick's hesitation. Then he muttered, "You didn't really like the snake, did you?"

"Nope."

"Are you sure?"

"I'm sure."

"Are you certain?"

"I'm certain."

Nick wouldn't leave it alone. "I realize I stuck my nose in where I had no business sticking it."

"True."

His hands were wrapped tensely around what she called the steering wheel. "I realize I may have gotten a little heavy-handed."

"Also true."

"It was for your own good," he growled, his mouth a thin line.

"So you informed me at the time."

"Do you believe I did it for your own good?"

She thought about it and answered, "I believe *you* thought you did."

Nick made some adjustment on the instrument panel in front of him. It was a minute, perhaps two, before he spoke again. "Are you sore at me?"

"For what?"

"Interfering."

"It's too late for regrets, don't you agree?"

He gave one emphatic nod of his head. "You are sore at me."

"That's not what I said."

"What did you say?"

Melina wasn't sure if she wanted to strangle the big galoot or kiss him until...

She cleared her throat. "I'll try to put it in plain, simple English. I have no interest in Hunter James. I never have. I never will. He's not my type. He wouldn't be my type in a million years. But I think it's cute that you're jealous."

That brought a minor explosion—as she had known it would.

"Jealous?" Nick roared.

"About my interest in another man," she explained as if he needed it explained.

"Cute?" he roared again.

Melina reached out and patted his muscular arm. "I must admit I'm surprised, too."

He appeared confused. "Surprised by what?"

"That you would do something, anything, that could remotely be described as cute."

His brows shot up. "I am not cute."

"I didn't say you were."

"I don't do cute things."

She gave a little private laugh. "That, of course, is a matter of opinion."

"It is not."

"It is, too." She glanced up and pointed with her finger. "Shouldn't you be watching out for those rocks?"

Nick's head swirled around and he swore fiercely. "Son of a—"

The boat lurched, then pitched from side to side as he maneuvered around the treacherous rocks and apparently found a safer route into the island of Pequeño.

"Are we there?" Melina asked. She decided it might be wise to drop the inflammatory subject of his cuteness.

"We're there."

She looked around. It wasn't noon yet—it wouldn't be for another two hours—but the blue mist was already rolling in from the sea. The island itself was small and green and lush, with rocky outcroppings at either end.

Nick had a copy of the map in one hand and the boat's wheel in the other. He cut the power by half and slowly trolled, searching for the cove clearly marked on the paper.

"There it is," he said, indicating an inlet straight ahead of them.

Melina felt the butterflies fluttering wildly in her stomach. "Where do we park?"

That raised a tawny eyebrow.

She tried again. "Where do we drop anchor?"

"We'll tie up along that stretch of beach."

Five minutes later they were ashore and sorting out their equipment.

Nick obviously thought he was in charge of the expedition. "We'll take only the gear we agreed on—food, water, shovel, lanterns, ponchos, rope and knapsacks."

Melina gave a smart salute. "Yessir!"

He didn't even blink. "Ready?"

"Ready."

"You're excited, aren't you?"

"Yes, I am."

"We're off."

She fell into step beside him. Nick seemed to realize that his legs were far longer and adjusted the pace accordingly.

"Thank you," she said, keeping up with him.

"You're welcome." Then it was strictly business. "Once we locate the opening of the cave, I go in first. If I decide it's safe for you to follow, I'll give a signal."

"No," she stated firmly.

"No what?"

Melina spit the words at him. "No, sir!"

"That's not what I meant." Nick waved military protocol aside. "I meant what do you mean by no?"

"Which part don't you understand?" she asked, feigning innocence. "The *n* or the *o?*"

"Very cute."

"I thought so."

The man was obviously used to having his orders followed without question. This would be a learning experience for him.

He was adamant. "You will stay outside."

She was determined. Shaking her head, she told him, "No can do."

"Melina—"

"Nick—"

He halted and dug the heels of his boots into the soft sand. "You are an exasperating, headstrong, independent-minded woman," he crabbed.

"Thank you."

"I didn't mean it as a compliment."

"I know." He had to understand. She poked his chest with her finger. "It is my map, Nick, my Grand Adventure, my pirate treasure. If there is any danger involved, I am not about to allow you to take chances that I'm not taking myself. We either both go in—" she blew out her breath and stood her ground "—or neither of us goes in."

He finally said, "I don't like it."

"You don't have to like it," she reminded him.

"If there's any trouble, you get your cute little butt out of there pronto."

"Is that an order?"

"Yes."

"I would, anyway." They started off down the beach. "The same goes for you."

"Huh?"

"If there's any trouble, you get *your* cute little butt out of there pronto."

Nick seemed to find that amusing. He was still chuckling softly as they approached the cave. It was overgrown with vines and vegetation. He took what appeared to be a small machete and hacked an opening large enough to walk through.

"Normally I would insist on 'ladies first,' but under the circumstances..."

He bent to avoid bumping his head on the top of the entrance. Melina was right behind him. In fact, when he stopped abruptly, she ran smack-dab into his back.

"Oomph!"

"You all right?"

"Yes," she hissed.

Once they were inside the cave, the opening widened. They could stand up straight, side by side.

"It's dark in here," she whispered.

"Give your eyes a chance to adjust to the dim light," he recommended.

"I still can't see a thing," she muttered.

"Why are you whispering?"

"It seemed like a good idea."

Nick turned on his lantern. She did the same. "Stay here until I've had a quick look around," he instructed in a no-nonsense tone.

Melina didn't stick her tongue out at him until he'd disappeared into the dark. He was back in less than three minutes. She knew because she'd had time to count to only one hundred and one.

"There is this entranceway and a larger cave just beyond it. They both seem dry and structurally sound."

"Now you're beginning to sound like an engineer."

"Thank you."

She hastened to tell him. "I didn't mean it as a compliment."

Nick grinned. "I know."

They walked into the cave. It was approximately the size of the living room at the cottage on Cayo Hazard: twenty feet by thirty feet. The ceiling was a good ten feet above their heads. The floor was sand. The walls and ceiling were stone.

"I thought the air would be stale," she said, taking a deep breath. "But it's not."

"There's fresh air coming in from somewhere," Nick agreed as he began to explore.

Melina could smell it. She could feel it stirring the tendrils around her face.

"It's just a plain old cave," she said later, somewhat disappointed.

"What did you expect?"

She kicked at a loose rock with her toe. "I guess I was hoping for a huge cavern with the mainsail of a frigate sticking halfway out of the water. Or a remote waterfall with a hidden entrance behind it. Or gold doubloons at the bottom of a crystal-clear pool. Or, at the very least, the stubble of a pirate's candle."

"You've been reading too many books."

She ignored his comment. "Heck, we don't even know if we're looking in the right cave."

"We are," Nick stated.

"What makes you so sure?"

He stood directly behind her and raised her arm along with his until they were pointing toward an opening overhead in the rocks.

"There."

"There *what?*"

"That's where the light comes in."

"That hole in the ceiling?"

"It's man-made."

"How can you tell?"

"B.S. in engineering. Graduate degree, Purdue University. Five years as a navy SEAL. Shall I go on?"

She shook her head. "I'll take your word for it."

"I can also see the ax marks."

Melina gave him a playful nudge with her elbow. Then she asked, "What time is it?"

"Eleven-thirty."

"A half hour."

"Plenty of time for us to get into place, and to synchronize our watches," he said.

Again?

"What will we do at blue noon?"

"I will mark the time. On the stroke of twelve you will draw a line in the sand that exactly corresponds to the shaft of light that enters through that hole."

Melina looked from the ceiling of the cave to the natural sand floor. "The treasure is buried under our feet."

"Somewhere."

"We can't just start digging."

"We'd be digging forever."

"We return tonight and mark where the light falls when the full moon is directly overhead. The two shafts of light should form an *X*. *X* marks the spot." She saw it all now.

"By jove, I think she's got it!"

"What do we do between noon and midnight?"

Nick threw an arm around her shoulders. "We have lunch. We explore the island. We take a nap." He brushed his hand back and forth along his chin. "Can you come *up* with anything else?" There was a knowing smirk on his handsome face.

Melina planted her hands on her hips. "Didn't anyone ever tell you that a pun is the lowest form of humor?"

"Nope."

"It is."

"I thought it was kind of—"

"Cute?"

Nick cleared his throat. "Time to synchronize our watches."

"We've got twenty minutes to go," she informed him. "By the way, what does the lettering on your cap stand for?"

"It's a little-known Slavic language."

"Yes?"

"There is no precise English translation."

"Imprecisely, then."

"In so many words..."

"You're stalling."

"You noticed."

"Are you embarrassed to tell me?"

Nick snapped his fingers together. "Yes. That's it, honey. Embarrassed."

Now she was getting muddled. "Are you embarrassed or are you embarrassing?"

He laughed out loud. The sound echoed off the walls of the cave. "There won't be a dull moment."

"Don't change the subject. I want to discuss your cap."

"We will," he promised.

"When?"

"Between lunchtime and naptime," Nick vowed.

Fourteen

"This place gives me the creeps." Melina shivered and pulled her cotton jacket closer around her.

"It's just a cave," Nick said reasonably.

"It's awfully dark in here."

"It was dark in here earlier today, too," he observed with typical male logic.

Melina didn't want logic, male or otherwise. She wanted sympathy and understanding. She wanted a strong arm around her shoulder and a warm hand holding hers.

"It nears the witching hour," she whispered.

"The what?"

"'Once upon a midnight dreary...'"

"The weatherman predicted clear skies and a brilliant full moon," he countered as they hauled their equipment through the opening and into the main chamber of the cave.

"'Of Cerberus and blackest Midnight born, in Stygian cave forlorn, 'mongst horrid shapes, and shrieks, and sights unholy,'" she quoted dramatically.

Nick narrowed his eyes. "I take it back."

"Take *what* back?"

"I said you weren't an actress. I was wrong." He paused. "In fact, you should be on the stage."

They delivered the punch line of the joke together. "And there's one leaving in five minutes."

Melina half laughed and half groaned, but the tension—which had been thick enough to cut with a knife—was relieved.

"I guess you've heard that one," he said.

"I guess I have."

"It's an old joke."

"Which reminds me of another old joke."

Nick adroitly cut her off. "We'd better get ready."

"It is ten minutes to twelve," Melina noted, and shivered again.

He slipped his free arm around her for a moment. "Don't worry, sweetheart, I'm here to take care of you."

"Thank God for small favors," she said dryly.

They positioned the unlit lanterns they'd brought with them in a wide circle around the perimeter of the cave.

"I have five minutes before the hour," Nick told her. "Do you have any questions?"

"Not a one."

"You've got to get it right the first time."

"I realize that."

"If you don't, it will be another year before there is a full moon in June."

"I understand."

"I don't want to make you nervous."

"You aren't."

"I just want you to know what you have to do."

"I know. I understand. I will."

"So, are you ready?"

"Good grief!"

"A simple 'yes, Nick,' will do."

"A simple and emphatic, 'yes, Nick!' "

As she had rehearsed under his tutelage several times—more like a dozen times—that afternoon, Melina took the small shovel and prepared herself. In the dark she could barely make out the mark she had drawn at noon. But she knew it was there, approximately fifteen feet long and three inches wide.

"Watch your feet," Nick admonished as he doused the last lantern.

"I am."

"Get ready," he said, consulting the illuminated dial on his watch.

"I'm ready."

"Counting down from ten seconds. Ten. Nine. Eight. Seven. Six. Five. Four. Three. Two. One."

Through the opening in the ceiling the light of the full moon came streaming into the cave. It cut a wide and distinct swath across the sandy floor. Melina quickly traced its pathway with the edge of her shovel. She could see already that the second line was going to intersect the first to form an unmistakable *X*.

"It's working, Nick!" she cried softly, her heart pounding in her breast. "It's working!"

"I know. I know." She could hear the excitement in his voice.

"I've got it." She finished and backed away, making sure she didn't step on the marks.

"Stay where you are," he instructed. "I'll relight the lanterns."

Several minutes later the cave was aglow with light. Nick drove a stake into the center of the *X*.

"Sunlight and moonlight," she murmured, amazed by their success.

"Sunlight and moonlight," he echoed. "And this is where I dig."

"Where *we* dig."

"In that case, you'd better put these on," he advised, handing her a pair of work gloves.

"Where are yours?"

He held up both hands. "Calluses."

They began. They shoveled sand and more sand and still more sand until they were both drenched in sweat.

"I didn't think it would be such hot work on such a cool evening," Melina commented as she stopped and stripped off her cotton jacket. She draped it over a natural rock formation that protruded from the cave wall. "How far down do you think we've gone?"

Nick pulled his T-shirt over his head and used it as a towel. "Three feet, maybe four."

"I wonder how deep we'll have to dig," she speculated aloud as she threw a shovelful over her shoulder.

"There's no way to tell."

"When I was a little girl I used to think if I dug a hole deep enough in our garden I'd end up on the other side of the world," she reminisced.

"I sure as hell hope we don't have to dig that far." Nick leaned on the handle. "I'll keep working. You take a break and drink some water. You don't want to get dehydrated."

"All right."

She was grateful for the rest. Her back was aching, and her arms were tired. Not that she intended to complain to Nick. The project had been her idea. It was her responsibility. Not his. Of course, she would never have gotten this far without his help, his expertise, his encouragement.

Melina watched the shadows play across the cave walls. Nick worked in the lantern light, his muscles flexing and his skin glistening with perspiration. She couldn't seem to take her eyes off him. Her gaze was riveted to his body.

Then he abruptly stopped.

She mopped her brow with a handkerchief. "Have you found something?"

"Not something." He hesitated. "Someone."

Suddenly her mouth was dry. "Someone?" She peered into the hole.

"It's a human skeleton," Nick stated.

She didn't want to ask, but she had to. "Does it have a—" she tried to swallow the lump in her throat "—head?"

He made a production of looking around him. "Yes, I'm sure it does. There must be a head around here somewhere."

"That's not funny, Nick."

"I didn't do it to be funny, sweetheart. I can't find the head. Oh, there it is."

"Don't touch it."

He glanced up at her. "The poor guy has been dead a long time, Melina. All that's left of him now are a few harmless bones."

"I don't care. It gives me the willies," she informed him. Her neck snapped around. "Did you hear that?"

"What?"

"That noise."

"No, I didn't."

"Well, I heard something."

"What kind of noise was it?" he inquired.

A chill coursed down Melina's spine. She lowered her voice to just above a whisper. "Moaning."

They waited, and they listened.

"It must have been the wind. There's no one here but the two of us," Nick finally said to her.

She exhaled. "I guess so."

"I know so."

"Whatever you say."

Nick respectfully avoided the skeleton and kept digging. He had excavated another foot of sand when his shovel hit something solid. "Bingo."

Her heart leaped. "It's the treasure chest."

"Keep calm, it may be nothing more than a rock."

But it wasn't a rock.

Lantern in hand, Melina hung over the pit they had dug and watched as Nick brushed the sand and dirt from a moldering old chest.

She tried to keep the dismay out of her voice. "It's a lot smaller than I'd imagined."

"It's a lot heavier than I'd imagined," Nick muttered as he lifted the chest from the hole.

He planted his hands in the sandy soil on either side of the excavation site and hoisted himself up. Then he went down on his haunches in front of the small trunk.

Melina squatted beside him. "It looks old."

Nick made a noncommittal sound. "Maybe."

"It could be seventeenth century."

"It could be."

"What do you think we'll find inside?"

He shook his head. "I don't know."

She reached out and placed a hand on his arm. "I know what you're afraid of, Nick."

He turned and stared into her eyes. "You do?"

"You're afraid I'll get my hopes up, only to have them dashed to the ground if the chest is empty, or filled with sand or rocks or funny money."

"Funny money?"

"You know, fake money. Counterfeit money."

"Ah." He reached out and tucked a loose strand of hair behind her ear. "I wouldn't want your Grand Adventure to prove a big disappointment, that's all."

"It won't. No matter what we find or don't find in the chest, this has been the most exciting two weeks of my life." Melina realized she meant every word.

The shadows closed around them.

"Think of how few people ever discover the treasure they're searching for," Nick said as he fiddled with the lock.

"The odds must be a million to one." She chewed on her lip. "A billion to one. Maybe even a trillion to one."

He summed it up neatly. "The odds are astronomical."

Melina watched as Nick pried the padlock open with his knife—in truth, the shackle was so rusty it practically fell off—and then the lid was ready to be raised.

"Take a deep breath," he ordered.

She did.

"Be careful not to cut yourself," he warned her.

She promised to be careful.

"The honor is all yours."

Melina lifted the lid and peered into the chest. Her hopes plummeted. There was nothing inside. "No Spanish doubloons," she announced.

"No Spanish doubloons."

"No strands of precious pearls."

"No precious pearls," he agreed.

"No gold chalices or priceless emeralds big enough to choke a horse."

"Nope. Not a one." His voice was perfectly level. "Aren't you going to see what's in the box?"

She looked again. There was a small nondescript box tucked into a shadowy corner of the chest. She picked it up and weighed it in her palm. "It's not heavy."

"Could be empty."

She shook her head. "It's not empty. I can tell something is moving inside."

"Moving?"

"There's a rattle."

"A rattle?"

"A short, sharp noise."

"I know what a rattle is."

She turned the box from one side to the other. "It looks like tin."

"Silver would be my guess," Nick offered.

"Very tarnished silver."

"You'd be tarnished, too, if you had spent the past three hundred years in a chest buried in the ground," he said readily.

That brought her head up. "Do you really think this is Sir Henry Morgan's treasure?"

"It's possible."

"Possible, but not probable."

Nick lifted his bare shoulders and dropped them again. "The odds are against it."

"Here goes." She tried to open the box. It wouldn't budge. "It's locked."

"I can take care of that," volunteered Nick, brandishing his small machete.

"I wonder..." Melina reached up and unhooked the chain she wore around her neck. She removed the small ornate key. "It opens the miniature chest I found in my grandparents' attic," she explained.

"It might work. There appear to be similarities between the two boxes."

"Here goes."

Inserting the key, Melina gave it a turn. Nothing happened. She tried again. This time she heard a distinct click. She heaved a sigh of relief and raised the lid.

They were sparkling.

They were clear.

Melina emptied the contents of the silver box into her hand. "Ohmigod!"

They were diamonds.

Stunned, they both crouched there for a moment without moving, without speaking. Then Melina slowly straightened, and Nick rose to stand beside her.

She stared at her hand. "Diamonds."

"You can say that again."

"There must be a small fortune in the palm of my hand."

"I'll be damned!" swore Nick.

"You cain say that again," came a rustic voice from behind them.

They both turned.

Melina's mouth dropped open. "It's the gargoyle."

"Conch, what the hell are you doing sneaking up on us?" Nick demanded to know.

"You ain't my boss," Conch claimed with a toothless smile as he pulled on the bill of his cap. "I do what I'm told."

"Who told you to sneak up on us?"

"Cain't tell."

He was starting to get that funny feeling in his gut. "Can't or won't?"

Conch stubbornly snapped his mouth shut.

But Nick was pretty sure he knew the answer. If he hadn't been so busy digging for buried treasure he would have noticed the godawful sensation sooner.

Melina dropped the diamonds back into the box and closed the lid. Then she pointed her finger at the handyman. "You were outside my bedroom window."

Conch guffawed.

Nick wanted a few other questions answered. "Where did you get the key to the cottage?"

"He gave it to me."

"Who's he?"

"Cain't tell you."

Melina interjected a query of her own. "Did you slip into the library one night and take a piece of scratch paper out of my wastebasket?"

The handyman wrinkled up his brow. It was obvious to Nick that he had no idea what she was talking about.

His gaze dropped to Conch's feet. "Nice boots you've got there."

Conch grinned from ear to ear. "Thanks."

"You must wear about a what? Size twelve?" he speculated.

Untrusting eyes grew even more wary. "You cain't have them. They're practically brand new. He gave them to me."

"Who gave them to you? Hunter James?"

Conch nodded his head.

Nick wanted to kick himself. He knew there had to be somebody with brains behind this, whatever *this* was. "I should have guessed—Hunter James the Third."

"You can say that again," came an icy-cold voice from behind Conch.

He swore softly. "Son of a bitch."

The second man stepped from the shadows into the light. "Well, doesn't this make a pretty picture?" Hunter James drawled. "Man. Woman. Diamonds." He held out the hand *without* the gun. "I'll take the diamonds."

Melina didn't move a muscle.

Nick started talking again. Stall tactics, that's what they called it in the business. "You took the scrap of paper from the cottage."

A nod of the handsome head. "Guilty as charged."

"Why?"

"To see what was written on it, of course," the polo player said, laughing. It was not a pleasant sound.

Nick was curious. "Why were you on Cayo Hazard in the first place?"

Black eyes narrowed to mere slits. "Why shouldn't I be on the island? It was in my family long before the Hazards had ever heard of the Florida Keys."

"Your family were the original owners?" Melina blurted out.

"Chalk up one for the lady librarian," he said sarcastically.

It had been Nick's experience that amateur crooks—and Hunter James definitely qualified as an amateur crook—loved to brag about their clever schemes. "What the hell are you up to?"

"Just trying to get a little of my own back. I've kept a close watch on the island and its inhabitants since you damned Hazards stole the place from us."

"We didn't steal it from you. The bank foreclosed, and Simon bought the island fair and square."

Hunter James chose to ignore the facts. "Revenge is sweet," he said, rocking back and forth on his heels.

"Revenge?" Nick mouthed. "Revenge for what? Your extravagant life-style? Your greed? Your stupidity?"

"That's enough," Hunter snapped testily. "I'll take the diamonds now." He brandished the pistol in his hand. "And no funny stuff, Hazard, or the lady gets it."

This time Melina moved. She handed over the silver box and quickly stepped back.

"Don't try to follow us," the snake warned. "Or you'll be sorry." He smiled humorlessly. "Not that you have anything to follow us *in*."

"What did you do to my boat?"

"Conch has taken care of your boat."

His partner in crime nodded his head. "I took care of the boat."

"He scuttled it."

Conch frowned. "Scuttled?"

Hunter James rolled his eyes. "Destroyed... as in drilled holes in the bottom of and sank in deep waters."

The handyman made a futile gesture. "You said get rid of it, Mr. James. So I got rid of it. You didn't say anything about drilling holes in the bottom and sinking it."

"What did you do to their boat?" came the impatient query.

"I gave it a good push."

"Which is probably what Hunter intends to do with you, Conch, once you stop being useful to him." Nick glanced down at his watch meaningfully. "Which I estimate will be in about fifteen minutes."

A scowl formed on the poor creature's face. "Huh?"

"Once you're in deep waters," Nick expounded.

"Shut up!" Hunter James barked. "Or I'll shut you up permanently. Maybe if you're lucky, Hazard, they'll find you and the lady before you run out of food and water." He shrugged his impeccably attired shoulders. "Then again, maybe they won't." He turned to his henchman. "Smash all of the lanterns but one."

Conch did as he was ordered. Then the two men began to back out of the cave, taking the only light with them.

Nick decided it was time for his parting shot. "By the way, I wouldn't worry about the curse if I were you."

Conch hesitated. "Curse? What curse?"

"The curse on the treasure of Sir Henry Morgan, of course. The unfortunate sailor chosen to protect the diamonds is still lying there in his grave. Headless. May God rest his soul. But don't let that bother you. Nobody believes in curses in this day and age."

"Nobody believes in curses," Melina piped up. "Although I swear I heard something or someone moan while we were digging in the sand, Nick."

"Did you, sweetheart?"

"Yes."

"That's enough," Hunter James said. "Get out now, Conch. I'll be right behind you." He held up the last unbroken lantern. "Adios, sucker."

As he left the cave Nick muttered, "Bastard."

The sound of Hunter James's self-satisfied laughter filtered back to them.

Melina called out. "Scurvy dog!"

Nick found her hand in the dark. "Scurvy dog?"

"It's an old pirate expression. It means 'you louse.'"

"I know what it means." He was disgusted with his own ineptness. "I blame myself. I should have seen it coming. I should have posted a guard."

"Who?"

"You." Nick dropped her hand and reached for his T-shirt. He pulled it on over his head. "I'm going to count to twenty. Then I intend to follow them."

"*We* will follow them."

"Melina—"

"Nick—"

"All right. *We* will follow them. But don't forget there's a full moon out tonight. Stay in the shadows. We don't know how good Hunter James is with that gun."

"Yessir!"

He found her hand again. "Ready, sweetheart?"

"Ready."

"Scared?"

She gave his hand a squeeze. "Not with you by my side."

They slipped from the cave and scooted behind a thick clump of vegetation. The moon shone brightly overhead, illuminating the water, the solitary boat some fifty yards offshore and the two men in it.

"There's something wrong," Melina whispered. "They appear to be arguing."

"Conch isn't as dense as he seems," Nick said with a genuine feeling of satisfaction.

"Nicholas Hazard, what have you done?"

"Psychological warfare."

"What?"

"I planted a seed or two of doubt in Conch's mind," he told her. "Is the treasure cursed? Does the ghost of the headless sailor guard the diamonds? Will Hunter James push him overboard once they reach the open sea?"

"It looks like Conch just grabbed the box of diamonds from Hunter," she said, giving him a play-by-play of the action as if he couldn't see it for himself.

"Maybe he thinks they should divvy up the treasure now," Nick offered.

"Hunter has rustled the diamonds back from Conch."

"By the way, when you closed the box in the cave, did you lock it again?"

"Nope."

"How sturdy was the catch?"

"It was hanging by a thread," she said.

They watched as the diamonds went back and forth between the two men. There were shouts of anger and cries of outrage, arm-waving and a few poorly thrown punches.

That's when it happened.

The lid of the silver box must have popped open. Suddenly there was a shower of sparkling diamonds flying through the air. They were suspended against the moonlit sky for a moment like tiny shooting stars. Then one by one they dropped into the sea and disappeared beneath the surface of the water.

Both men dived for the treasure and missed. The boat rocked back and forth precariously. Then it gave a final heave and flipped over, spilling its passengers into the cold abyss. A moment later two heads bobbed above the water.

"Oops!" Nick said in classic understatement.

Melina turned and looked at him. "Oops?"

Nick gazed down at her lovely face. "Oops. It's a common expression which, roughly translated from the original English, means 'oh, dear.'"

Melina chuckled. "I know what it means."

He ran his eyes over her for any signs of distress. "Do you mind too much?"

"About what?"

"The diamonds."

"I don't mind as much as I thought I would." She shrugged her slender shoulders. "Easy come. Easy go."

"Speak for yourself, Miss Morgan. My back is killing me." She stepped closer, reached around him and began to massage the muscles just above his waist. He was tempted to groan with pure pleasure. Instead he reminded her, "Not that we don't have bigger problems."

Her eyes dropped.

Nick put his hand under her chin and lifted. "Not that kind of problem, honey. We have to find a way to get off this island pronto. I would prefer not to share Pequeño with Hunter James and Conch."

"Then you are—we are—in luck."

"We are?"

Melina was staring at something over his right shoulder. He turned around. Twenty yards down the sandy moonlit beach their boat was washing ashore.

"Thank God Conch is incompetent."

"Maybe he was incompetent," Melina called softly as they ran for their transport off the pirate island. "Or maybe there really was a curse on Sir Henry Morgan's God-given treasure."

Fifteen

"I never thought I would say this, but Bloody Mary's seafood chowder really hits the spot," Melina confessed as she upturned the thermos. There wasn't a drop left. She overcame her genuine disappointment and told Nick, "It was sure nice of Mary to bring us something to eat while we were filling out the official police reports."

"Yes, it was."

She leaned toward him and lowered her voice to a confidential level. "Mary Worthwyle knows absolutely everything about everybody on Key West."

"No."

"Yes." Melina lowered her volume another decibel or two. "Do you know what she confided in me?"

Nick sank into the chair beside her. "What did she confide to you?"

"She heard it from a very reliable source."

"What other kind is there?"

"Mary told me that Penelope James—" She stopped and digressed for a minute. "That's Hunter James's stepmother, by the way. She was married to Hunter James the Second at the time of his death. Penelope was his fourth wife."

"Fourth wife, huh?"

"She's known in these parts as Peacock Penelope."

"Don't tell me," Nick claimed. "She imported the peacocks to Cayo Hazard."

Melina nodded her head. "Of course, it wasn't Cayo Hazard at the time. Anyway, Mary heard that Penelope James has a new suitor."

"A suitor?"

"A beau. A male admirer."

"I know what a suitor is."

She went on with her story. "The woman has given up brandy and bridge, and has moved with her beau to the Bahamas."

"Why the Bahamas?"

"I knew you were going to ask that question," she responded smugly. "It just so happens that the man owns an island in the Bahamas."

"An amazing story."

"It is, isn't it?" She screwed the lid back on the empty thermos. "What about Hunter James and Conch?"

"The Coast Guard is already on its way to Pequeño." Nick rubbed his hand back and forth along his chin. "The archaeologists won't be far behind."

"Archaeologists?"

"There may be something of interest to them in the cave."

Melina heaved a sigh. "I was hoping it could all be laid to rest."

"It will be." Nick stood and held out his hand to her. "Are you ready to go home?"

"Yes. Let's go home."

It was not without a pang of regret, however, that she said the word *home.* Her vacation was nearly over and soon she would be going home to Wisconsin.

Wisconsin.

It seemed like a lifetime ago. Which was real? An island paradise off the coast of Florida or the small town she had lived in her entire twenty-nine years?

Maybe they both were real.

"Your place or mine?" Nick asked an hour later as they tied up the boat and headed down the path toward the cottages.

"Since the cottages are essentially identical except for the color..."

"Yours."

She was curious. "Why?"

"It's closer."

"What did you tell the police about the diamonds?" Melina inquired as she unlocked the door of the pink cottage.

"I told them the truth. I said that the diamonds were now scattered to the four winds...or to the seven seas, as the case may be."

She opened the door and went inside. "Just think of it. Perhaps a hundred years from now, halfway around the world, another treasure hunter may find one of those diamonds." The prospect cheered her greatly. "I like that idea. I've had my Grand Adventure. Next time it will be someone else's turn."

Nick hovered on the front porch as he had that first night. "No regrets?"

It suddenly occurred to Melina that he was asking her an important question. It wasn't just about diamonds. "I don't regret one thing I've done since I arrived on Cayo Hazard," she told him. "Are you coming in?"

"I thought you'd never ask." He stepped into the hallway and closed the door behind him.

She headed for the kitchen. He was at her heels. "I ate most of the seafood chowder. Are you hungry?"

"Starved."

"You sure know how to work up an appetite, don't you?" she commented, placing six slices of bread on the table and spreading them with mustard.

Appetite.

His appetite for her was insatiable. But, Nick realized as he watched Melina slice ham and cheese for their sandwiches, it wasn't just physical.

He couldn't seem to get enough of her smiles, her laughter, her crazy sense of humor, her Caribbean blue eyes, the way she watched him when she didn't know he was watching her.

He couldn't get enough of her soft cries of ecstasy, the way she whimpered his name, the touch of her cool hands on his hot flesh, the feel of her, the taste of her, the scent of her.

How could he let her go?

How could he allow Melina to walk out of his life and never see her again?

It hit Nick like a ton of bricks. He couldn't let her go. He couldn't allow her to walk away. He couldn't imagine his life without her in it.

He was in love with Melina.

Somehow, some way, while he wasn't paying attention, Melina Morgan had found her way into his heart and soul. She was his. She would always be his. He must make certain of that.

"Do you like Wisconsin?" Nick blurted out.

Melina glanced up from her sandwich making. "Do I like Wisconsin?"

"Yes or no?"

"Yes."

"How about Moose Creek?"

"I've lived there since the day I was born."

"That doesn't mean you like it, and that doesn't mean you want to spend the rest of your life in the place," he observed logically.

"True."

"Well, do you?"

"Do I what?"

"Do you want to spend the rest of your life in Moose Creek?" he asked.

"As compared to where?"

Nick plucked the name of a city out of the air. "Chicago."

"I've been to Chicago several times," she said noncommittally. "It seems like a very nice city."

"It is." He began to extol Chicago's virtues. "We have the Art Institute, the Field Museum, the Shedd Aquarium, plenty of shopping, restaurants, cultural opportunities and libraries. Chicago has dozens of libraries. A hundred libraries. Maybe a thousand libraries."

"An astronomical number?" she supplied.

"Precisely. There would be more books than even *you* could read in a lifetime."

Melina came to a dead stop, the kitchen knife suspended in midair, the mustard slowly dripping plop, plop, plop onto the table. "What are you trying to say, Nick?"

Nick pushed his chair back and stood. He removed the knife from her hand and laid it down. Then he pulled Melina into his arms and gazed down into her face. "I'm trying to tell you that I want to be your Prince Charming, your knight on a white charger, your Sir what's-his-name."

"Sir Galahad," she said and laughed softly, somewhere in the back of her throat.

"There."

"There?"

"That's one of the things I love about you—the way you laugh."

She stiffened in his arms.

Nick frowned. "Did I say something wrong?"

She shook her head.

"Did I say something right?"

She shook her head again.

"Well, if it's not wrong and it's not right, then what is it, honey?"

He watched as the tears emerged from Melina's eyes and clung to her dark, spiky lashes. She muttered something that he didn't quite catch. "What?"

"It's—it's perfect," she blubbered.

"What is?"

"You are."

"That's nice of you to say, sweetheart, but I'm far from perfect. Every man has his faults."

"That's not what I meant."

"What did you mean, then?"

"You're perfect for me," she finally managed to get out.

"I know." Nick bent and brushed his lips back and forth across hers. "And you, Melina, are perfect for me."

"I am?"

Nick nodded. "I can't imagine kissing anyone but you. I can't imagine touching anyone but you, caressing anyone but you, making love to anyone but you." He took a deep breath. "I can't imagine loving anyone but you."

She mumbled something unintelligible.

"What was that?"

"Me, neither."

"Then it's settled."

"What's settled?"

"I love you. You love me. We're getting married, and we are going to live happily ever after," he declared.

Melina rested her head against his chest, wrapped her arms tightly around his waist and sighed with what he recognized as contentment.

"This has been the adventure of a lifetime," she told him.

Nick raised her lovely face to his. "Darling, the adventure is just beginning...."

* * * * *

A Word About Diamonds . . .

Diamonds are the hardest known substance. The only thing that will cut a diamond is another diamond. There have been many famous diamonds throughout history. "The Mountain of Light" has the oldest verifiable record of all diamonds and has been traced to 1304. It was purchased by Britain in 1849 and is now in the Queen Mother's crown. The recut stone weighs approximately 108 carats.

Diamonds are said to bring good fortune, and to endow the possessor with superior strength, courage and reproductive powers.

* * * * *

Look for Simon Hazard's story—the next installment of Hazards, Inc.—coming in 1995, only from Silhouette Desire!

INDULGE A LITTLE 6947 SWEEPSTAKES
NO PURCHASE NECESSARY

HERE'S HOW THE SWEEPSTAKES WORKS:

The Harlequin Reader Service shipments for January, February and March 1994 will contain, respectively, coupons for entry into three prize drawings: a trip for two to San Francisco, an Alaskan cruise for two and a trip for two to Hawaii. To be eligible for any drawing using an Entry Coupon, simply complete and mail according to directions.

There is no obligation to continue as a Reader Service subscriber to enter and be eligible for any prize drawing. You may also enter any drawing by hand printing your name and address on a 3" x 5" card and the destination of the prize you wish that entry to be considered for (i.e., San Francisco trip, Alaskan cruise or Hawaiian trip). Send your 3" x 5" entries to: Indulge a Little 6947 Sweepstakes, c/o Prize Destination you wish that entry to be considered for, P.O. Box 1315, Buffalo, NY 14269-1315, U.S.A. or Indulge a Little 6947 Sweepstakes, P.O. Box 610, Fort Erie, Ontario L2A 5X3, Canada.

To be eligible for the San Francisco trip, entries must be received by 4/30/94; for the Alaskan cruise, 5/31/94; and the Hawaiian trip, 6/30/94. No responsibility is assumed for lost, late or misdirected mail. Sweepstakes open to residents of the U.S. (except Puerto Rico) and Canada, 18 years of age or older. All applicable laws and regulations apply. Sweepstakes void wherever prohibited.

For a copy of the Official Rules, send a self-addressed, stamped envelope (WA residents need not affix return postage) to: Indulge a Little 6947 Rules, P.O. Box 4631, Blair, NE 68009, U.S.A.

INDR93

INDULGE A LITTLE 6947 SWEEPSTAKES
NO PURCHASE NECESSARY

HERE'S HOW THE SWEEPSTAKES WORKS:

The Harlequin Reader Service shipments for January, February and March 1994 will contain, respectively, coupons for entry into three prize drawings: a trip for two to San Francisco, an Alaskan cruise for two and a trip for two to Hawaii. To be eligible for any drawing using an Entry Coupon, simply complete and mail according to directions.

There is no obligation to continue as a Reader Service subscriber to enter and be eligible for any prize drawing. You may also enter any drawing by hand printing your name and address on a 3" x 5" card and the destination of the prize you wish that entry to be considered for (i.e., San Francisco trip, Alaskan cruise or Hawaiian trip). Send your 3" x 5" entries to: Indulge a Little 6947 Sweepstakes, c/o Prize Destination you wish that entry to be considered for, P.O. Box 1315, Buffalo, NY 14269-1315, U.S.A. or Indulge a Little 6947 Sweepstakes, P.O. Box 610, Fort Erie, Ontario L2A 5X3, Canada.

To be eligible for the San Francisco trip, entries must be received by 4/30/94; for the Alaskan cruise, 5/31/94; and the Hawaiian trip, 6/30/94. No responsibility is assumed for lost, late or misdirected mail. Sweepstakes open to residents of the U.S. (except Puerto Rico) and Canada, 18 years of age or older. All applicable laws and regulations apply. Sweepstakes void wherever prohibited.

For a copy of the Official Rules, send a self-addressed, stamped envelope (WA residents need not affix return postage) to: Indulge a Little 6947 Rules, P.O. Box 4631, Blair, NE 68009, U.S.A.

INDR93

INDULGE A LITTLE SWEEPSTAKES

OFFICIAL ENTRY COUPON

This entry must be received by: JUNE 30, 1994
This month's winner will be notified by: JULY 15, 1994
Trip must be taken between: AUGUST 31, 1994-AUGUST 31, 1995

YES, I want to win the 3-Island Hawaiian vacation for two. I understand that the prize includes round-trip airfare, first-class hotels and pocket money as revealed on the "wallet" scratch-off card.

Name________________________________

Address ____________________ Apt. __________

City________________________________

State/Prov.________________ Zip/Postal Code__________

Daytime phone number________________________
(Area Code)

Account #______________________________

Return entries with invoice in envelope provided. Each book in this shipment has two entry coupons—and the more coupons you enter, the better your chances of winning!

 MONTH3

INDULGE A LITTLE SWEEPSTAKES

OFFICIAL ENTRY COUPON

This entry must be received by: JUNE 30, 1994
This month's winner will be notified by: JULY 15, 1994
Trip must be taken between: AUGUST 31, 1994-AUGUST 31, 1995

YES, I want to win the 3-Island Hawaiian vacation for two. I understand that the prize includes round-trip airfare, first-class hotels and pocket money as revealed on the "wallet" scratch-off card.

Name________________________________

Address ____________________ Apt. __________

City________________________________

State/Prov.________________ Zip/Postal Code__________

Daytime phone number________________________
(Area Code)

Account #______________________________

Return entries with invoice in envelope provided. Each book in this shipment has two entry coupons—and the more coupons you enter, the better your chances of winning!

© 1993 HARLEQUIN ENTERPRISES LTD. MONTH3